"Why did you get engaged to him when you didn't love him?"

"I'm fond of Christos—it seemed a good idea."

Max laughed harshly. "A good idea? You mean your father pushed you into it, and Christos's father pushed him—they're using both of you, ruthlessly. Your marriage is the cement in the unholy alliance between my half brother and your father. They don't trust each other, with good reason, so they've each offered up a child, as a hostage for good behavior." He looked into her eyes. "That's the truth, isn't it, Olivia?"

Dear Reader,

The Seven Deadly Sins are those sins which most of us
are in danger of committing every day, very ordinary
failings, very human weaknesses, but which can cause
pain both to ourselves and others. Over the ages, they
have been defined as: Anger, Covetousness, Envy,
Greed, Lust, Pride and Sloth.

In this book, I deal with the sin of Covetousness. To
covet is to begrudge someone else's possessions, to
hanker after things owned by someone else. At some
time or another, don't we all wish we were millionaires
or had a wardrobe full of designer clothes? Though
daydreams are harmless, it is very different when a plot
is hatched to take something valuable away from its
rightful owner.

Charlotte Lamb

This is the second story in Charlotte Lamb's
gripping new series. Watch every month for five more
romances—all complete stories in themselves—where
this exceptionally talented writer proves that love can
conquer the deadliest of sins!

Coming next month: HAUNTED DREAMS (Harlequin
Presents #1828)...the sin of Envy. Have you ever felt
that the grass was greener on the other side?

ALSO AVAILABLE FROM HARLEQUIN PRESENTS

SINS
1816—SECRET OBSESSION: the sin of Pride

Charlotte Lamb

Deadly Rivals

Harlequin Books

TORONTO • NEW YORK • LONDON
AMSTERDAM • PARIS • SYDNEY • HAMBURG
STOCKHOLM • ATHENS • TOKYO • MILAN
MADRID • WARSAW • BUDAPEST • AUCKLAND

ISBN 0-373-11822-8

DEADLY RIVALS

First North American Publication 1996.

Copyright © 1995 by Charlotte Lamb.

This edition published by arrangement with Harlequin Books S.A.

® and TM are trademarks of the publisher. Trademarks indicated with
® are registered in the United States Patent and Trademark Office, the
Canadian Trade Marks Office and in other countries.

Printed in U.S.A.

CHAPTER ONE

THE little beach below her father's villa was private and lay at the end of a long, narrow, winding, rocky road which could only be reached through the villa gardens. In the early mornings, the beach was always empty, a stretch of white sand and rocks, with a thin belt of pine trees fringing it, and Olivia went down each day before breakfast to swim in the warm blue sea, feeling like Eve in the Garden of Eden, but without the serpent or Adam. She never had company. Her father didn't get up until much later, and any guests he had seemed to sleep late too.

Olivia loved the feel of the cool morning air on her skin as she wandered down the stony path, in her rope-soled sandals and sleek-fitting black swimsuit, hearing the murmur of the sea and the cry of gulls.

This morning a wave of such happiness broke over her that as she reached the beach she began cartwheeling over the sand, her smooth-skinned body supple in flowing movement.

A moment later she heard a harsh Greek voice shouting somewhere nearby, then the sound of running feet on the sand. Olivia was about to stand up when another body hit her violently.

The breath knocked out of her, she collapsed on the sand on her back with a man on top of her. A totally naked man.

Olivia screamed.

A hand hit her mouth, pressed down to silence her, muffling her cries. Olivia struggled against the bare male flesh, panic inside her.

Her golden-brown eyes huge, she threw a scared look up at him. He was big and powerful—that was her first impression. Wide, tanned shoulders, a muscled chest, flat stomach: it was an athlete's body. His colouring was Greek to match that deep voice: he had black hair, dusted with powdery sand at the moment, an olive-skinned face, glittering black eyes.

He stared back, those eyes narrowing, his winged black brows arching in sardonic comment.

'Blonde hair,' he said in English. 'A peaches-and-cream complexion...you have to be Faulton's daughter!'

Then his strong-featured face tightened in a grimace. 'Sorry if I startled you. Now don't scream again, there is no need to be alarmed. I'm not going to hurt you.' He took his hand away from her mouth and rolled off her at the same time, getting to his feet.

Olivia scrambled up too, sick with relief, shaking slightly, and beginning to get angry because she had been so frightened.

'Why did you do that?' she almost shouted at him.

He had his back to her. For all her anger, she couldn't help noticing how smooth and golden that back was: long, muscled, with a deep indentation running down the centre. He was winding a big white towel around his waist. Against the whiteness his skin was an even deeper tan, small dark hairs roughening his forearms and calves.

She looked away, swallowing on a sudden physical awareness, a pulse beginning to beat in her throat as she remembered that body lying on top of her, the forced intimacy of the brief contact.

He turned and looked at her coolly. 'You were about to crash into those rocks.'

Crossly she snapped, 'Nothing of the kind! I knew they were there! I was just going to change course to avoid them.'

His brows rose again. 'It didn't look to me as if you were.'

'Well, I was! I know every inch of this beach. If you hadn't interfered I would have veered to the right and gone on down into the sea.'

Just behind him she saw a pile of clothes on the rocks: crumpled, well-washed jeans, a cheap cotton T-shirt.

She looked back at him, frowning. 'Who are you? What are you doing on this beach anyway? It's private. Have you got permission to be here?'

'I'm staying at your father's villa. I arrived late last night, after you had gone to bed. Your father told me you were staying here too.'

She had gone to bed early; she always did, so that she could be up at first light. Olivia hated missing a moment of the morning here. It was the best time of day; each dawn was like the birth of the world—radiant, clear, breathtaking.

'My father didn't tell me anyone else was arriving,' she slowly said, running a still shaky hand through her short hair, which was cut in a bell shape, soft and silky like the petals of a yellow chrysanthemum, around her small, oval face. Olivia was only five feet four, and proportioned accordingly, with tiny hands and feet, a slender, fine-boned body. Her eyes were big, however, and wide-spaced, and her mouth was soft and generous, with something passionate in the warm curves of it.

The stranger's mouth was wide, too, but hard, the line of it uncompromising, forceful. 'I dropped in unex-

pectedly,' he said, and suddenly smiled, if you could call
the twist of that mouth a smile. Something was amusing
him, but that smile made a shiver run down her back.

'Where from? Do you live on Corfu?' Her father's
guests were usually rich businessmen and their wives—
people she tried to avoid as much as possible, and who
were often openly surprised, and curious, about her
presence, because few people knew that Gerald Faulton
had a child.

His marriage to her mother had ended in divorce when
Olivia was six and she had remained in her mother's
custody afterwards, growing up in a small town in
Cumbria, in the north-west of England. Gerald Faulton
had remarried once the divorce was final, only to divorce
again some years later, without having another child.
He had been married four times now, but Olivia was still
his only child, although they were hardly close; he didn't
keep in touch with her, except to send her a birthday
and Christmas present each year, usually some expensive yet impersonal gift she suspected was chosen by his
secretary. The only time they spent together was this
fortnight every year in his Corfu villa, and even then he
often had other guests to stay and saw very little of
Olivia.

The dark Greek eyes were watching her small mobile
face intently and she felt the skin on the back of her
neck prickle. Surely her thoughts didn't show in her face?
It always made her sad to think of her father; she did
not want this stranger guessing at her feelings.

But his voice was calm when he answered her. 'No, I
don't live here. I sailed here. My boat is down in the
harbour at Corfu Town.'

'You sail?' Olivia's golden eyes glowed with interest at that. 'I sail too. What size is your boat? Did you sail her single-handed, or do you have a crew?'

'I sailed single-handed—the boat's designed to be easy for one person to handle,' he said, giving her a shrewd look. 'Do you sail?'

'Not here, back home. I live in the Lake District, in England.'

He smiled, teeth very white against that deeply tanned skin. 'A lovely part of the country.'

'Oh, yes,' she said with fervour. 'Do you know it?'

He nodded, then, before she could ask him any more questions, he turned away, picked up his clothes and began to walk up the beach towards the pines behind which lay the white-walled villa.

Over his shoulder he said, 'Have your swim. See you later.'

Olivia watched him walk away, a tall, swift-moving man, the white towel flapping against his naked brown legs. Who was he? He hadn't told her his name or anything about himself, and she was consumed with curiosity, but it would have to wait until she met him again later back at the villa.

She turned and ran down into the sea, her body graceful as it dived through the blue water. Olivia swam like a fish. Her Cumbrian home was on the shores of one of the lakes which were the major tourist attraction in that part of England. She spent most of her leisure time on the water, sailing her small yacht, *White Bird*, and she had learned to swim at around the time she learned to walk. Her mother was a sports teacher at a local school and very keen on children learning to swim early, especially if they lived near water.

Olivia cut short her usual time on the beach that morning, but it was an hour later when she walked out on to the marble-tiled terrace where breakfast was eaten every morning in the shadow of the vines growing overhead. She had showered after her swim, her layered blonde hair was faintly damp, and she was wearing blue and white striped shorts which left most of her long, golden-brown legs bare, and a sleeveless yellow cotton top with a scalloped neckline.

Her father was at the table, reading yesterday's English newspapers, drinking coffee, having eaten his usual slice of toast and English marmalade, no doubt. Gerald Faulton was a man of ingrained habit, and disliked any changes to his routine.

He looked round the paper and gave her his abstracted smile, which always made her wonder if he really knew quite who she was and what she was doing in his house.

'Ah...good morning! Sleep well?' A well-preserved fifty-five-year-old, her father's once fair hair was now a silvery shade but his features were still as clear-cut and firm as ever because he dieted rigorously and exercised every day. His eyes were a piercing blue, a little cold, very sharp.

'Very well. Did you?'

'Yes. Been down to the beach, have you?' Gerald approved of his daughter's early rising and swimming, as he did of her glowing health and physical fitness.

'Yes. You should come down, Father. It's wonderful first thing in the morning.'

'I swam in the pool, as usual.' He didn't quite trust the sea. The water in his swimming pool was treated and 'safe'; there were no crashing waves to overwhelm you either.

Olivia never kissed her father; their relationship was far too distant for that. She smiled at him though, as she sat down opposite him, her golden eyes glowing with leonine warmth, but only got back that blank stare, as if Gerald Faulton found it hard to believe she was really his child.

Sighing a little, Olivia took one of the crisp, home-baked rolls put out in a silver basket in the centre of the table by the housekeeper, Anna Speralides, who looked after the villa whenever Gerald Faulton wasn't using it. Spreading the roll with home-made black cherry jam, she said casually, 'I met someone on the beach this morning. He said he was staying here, but he didn't tell me his name.'

Her father looked up, eyes alert. 'A Greek?'

'He spoke English fluently, but with a Greek accent.'

Gerald Faulton nodded. 'Max Agathios. Yes, he arrived late last night, unexpectedly.' He spoke in a clipped tone, his lips barely parting, and was frowning; she got the impression he was annoyed about the unannounced arrival.

Yet he had invited the man to stay. Olivia wondered why, but knew better than to ask. Her father did not like her to ask questions.

Max, she thought, remembering the hard, dark face. It suited him. She had wondered what his name would be, thought of all the Greek names she could remember...Achilles, Agamemnon, Odysseus...but had to giggle at the idea of him being called anything like that.

'Max doesn't sound Greek,' she thought aloud, tentatively watching her father.

For once Gerald Faulton seemed to be in a conversational mood. He shrugged. 'He was given his father's

name—Basil, I believe—one of the major Greek saints,
St Basil—but while old Agathios lived, to avoid confusion, they called the boy Max, which was his second
name. I think he got that from his mother's father.'
Gerald paused, frowning. 'I did once hear that his
mother's family were Austrian. I must ask him. Max's
mother was a second wife. The first one died. She was
Greek; she had a son, Constantine, then a few years later
I gather she died in childbirth and old Agathios married
again—a very beautiful woman, Maria Agathios—and
Max was born.'

Her father seemed to know a good deal about the
family. They must be wealthy, or important, or he
wouldn't be interested in them. The cynical little thought
made Olivia bite her lip. Her father wasn't that obsessed
with wealth. It was simply that his mind was one-track,
and business was what he lived for—if you weren't involved in his business he wasn't interested in you. Even
if you were his own daughter.

She looked down at her breakfast and suddenly didn't
want it; she pushed the plate away.

'Agathios,' she murmured, for something to say, and
the name suddenly rang a bell. 'Aren't they in shipping
too?' They would be, of course. What else had she
expected?

Gerald Faulton gave her an impatient look. 'They certainly are.' His voice had a snap. 'You should have
recognised the name at once. I thought you had.'

She had offended him again; she was expected to know
all about his company, and the other companies who
were his competitors and rivals, both in the United
Kingdom and worldwide.

He was frowning coldly. 'I thought you did business
studies at school? Don't they teach you the names of

the major shipping companies? Even if they don't, it would be the easiest matter in the world for you to find out for yourself, for heaven's sake! You might take an interest in my business. After all, one day you'll inherit my shares in the company! I don't have anyone else to leave them to!'

Angrily, he flapped his newspaper and went back behind it, instantly removed from her, absorbed once more into his normal world of business and finance.

Olivia wanted to shout at him that of course she knew all about his business! He had made sure of that, badgering her mother to put her through a business studies course at school and ever since sending her company brochures, talking to her endlessly about the company whenever she saw him, even though they spent so little time together. She had grown up with the subject permanently rammed down her throat.

Her father was the managing director of a British shipping line, Grey-Faulton, which had been built up after the Second World War by Gerald's father, Andrew, who had married the daughter of John Grey, who owned a rather run-down ferry business operating around Scotland. Andrew Faulton had built this into a thriving shipping business, expanding from ferries into freight, and in due course Gerald had inherited it all. Olivia had barely known her grandfather, who had died when she was ten, but she knew from what her mother had told her that Gerald had modelled himself on his father. 'I sometimes think that that ruthless old man was the only human being your father ever truly loved,' her mother had once said. Certainly the business was her father's driving obsession.

She should have guessed that the man she met on the beach was somehow involved in shipping from the fact that, for once, her father had talked so freely.

Sighing, Olivia felt the coffee-pot; it was lukewarm, but before she could ring for more coffee, her father's housekeeper brought it, smiling at the girl as she put down the heavy silver pot.

'Oh, fresh coffee...thank you! A lovely morning again, isn't it, Anna?' Olivia said, smiling back at her.

'Beautiful day,' agreed Anna. 'I heard you coming downstairs, so I brought more coffee. Do you want toast?'

Her English was very good, but her accent was Corfiot; she had been born here. A woman of nearly forty, she was faintly plump, with long, oiled black hair which she wore wound on top of her head, warm olive skin, big dark eyes and a full, glowing pink mouth. Anna had the beauty of her island—fertile, sun-ripened, inviting. Olivia had met her every year for twelve years, ever since Anna took over managing the villa. Anna's husband had worked there too, part-time. They had lived in a little annexe at the side of the villa, and Spiro had also been a fisherman. A few winters ago he had died in a storm, when his boat was lost, and there had been sadness in Anna's big, dark eyes for some years, but today it seemed to Olivia that Anna was more cheerful, almost her old self again.

'No, no toast, thanks, Anna,' Olivia carefully said in Greek; she only knew a few words but each year she managed to add a little more to her vocabulary because she liked to help Anna in the kitchen, learning Greek cooking and the Greek language at the same time.

Anna laughed. 'You're getting a better accent, Olivia,' she answered, in Greek.

The phone began to ring in the villa and Anna hurried off to answer it, returning a moment later to say to Gerald, 'It is for you. A Greek voice—he said to tell you Constantine. From London. Shall I put it through to your study?'

He got up, nodding, and followed Anna back into the house, leaving Olivia to finish her breakfast alone.

Constantine? she thought—hadn't her father mentioned that name just now? Oh, yes, Max Agathios had a brother called Constantine. Why was her father seeing so much of these Greek brothers? What was going on?

She had just finished her second cup of coffee when Max Agathios walked out on to the terrace. He was in his old jeans and T-shirt, but somehow they did not look shabby and disreputable on him. He managed to invest them with a sort of glamour, thought Olivia, staring at him.

He nodded to her. 'Where's your father?'

'On the phone to your brother,' she said, before she thought twice, and he gave her a quick, narrowed glance.

'My brother?'

Uncertainly, Olivia said, 'Well, I don't know that, I just assumed ... It's someone called Constantine.'

'Ringing from Piraeus?'

'No, London.' Olivia was worried now. Would her father be angry if he found out that she had told Max Agathios about this phone call?

'Ah.' Max turned and stared out towards the misty blue mountains on the horizon, the heat haze between them and the villa making them shimmer as if they were a mirage. A moment later he turned, his face calm. 'Well, I'll see him later. I'm going down to Corfu Town to check up on my boat. I needed some work done on the radio and I want to make sure it has been done properly.'

'I'd love to see your boat!' Olivia said wistfully.

'Well, come with me,' he said, at once. 'If you don't mind riding pillion on my motorbike.'

She was taken aback. 'You ride a motorbike? Did you hire it here?'

'No, I always have it on my boat. It's more convenient to have your own transport, wherever you end up!'

'Yes, it must be.' Olivia flushed with excitement. 'I've never ridden on a motorbike—I've always wanted to though!' Yet she didn't dare leave without asking her father's permission. Gerald was unpredictable; he might not approve of her going off with Max Agathios, and she might return to find him icily angry with her. Olivia found her father far too alarming to risk that. She had never learned how to talk to him, or cope with his moods, except by keeping quiet and out of his way.

Anna came out to clear the table and Max Agathios turned to speak to her in Greek. Olivia watched them both, wondering what he was saying, what Anna was answering. Anna smiled at him and Olivia thought, She likes him! She had never seen Anna smile at her father like that. Anna's olive-dark eyes had a lustre and a gleam that Olivia recognised, instinctively, as sensual. Anna found Max Agathios attractive; she was responding to him as a woman to a man she wanted, and Max smiled back at her with an unhidden appreciation of Anna's ripe warmth.

Olivia looked down, feeling excluded, left out, like a child at a grown-up party.

'OK, we can go—Anna will explain where we've gone,' Max said, startling her by suddenly being closer than she had thought.

She looked up, her skin pink, her eyes bothered, and he gave her a mocking little smile, as if he knew what had disturbed her and was amused by her reaction.

Anna had gone. They were alone on the terrace. Olivia hesitated, biting her lower lip, but why should her father object? He took very little interest in what she did while she was staying here, and if he disapproved of Max surely he wouldn't let him stay at the villa?

'Will I be OK dressed like this?' she uncertainly asked, and Max ran his eyes down over her slender figure in the brief striped shorts, the thin yellow top. That look made her breathless suddenly.

His brows lifted.

'Don't wear much, do you?'

'I didn't notice you wearing much on the beach this morning, either!' retorted Olivia, and he grinned at her wickedly.

'I wasn't expecting company. Well, come on! My motorbike is in the garage.'

They walked round to the front of the villa and went into the spacious garage, which usually just contained the bright red sports car her father had hired at the start of his holiday, as he did every year. Today it held a motorbike too; Max wheeled out the gleaming black machine, which was obviously new, streamlined and light, for easy transport on the boat, no doubt. Max picked up the black and yellow crash helmet which had been left on the leather saddle and held it out to her.

'Put this on.'

She hesitated. 'What about you?'

'I'm borrowing a spare one from the gardener,' he said with amusement, shouldering into a black leather jacket.

She had seen the gardener coming to work on his old bike, wearing a scratched and battered helmet, and laughed at the idea of Max wearing it.

As she began fumbling with the straps of his helmet he pushed her hands aside and adjusted them for her, his long, deft fingers cool on her flushed skin. The black leather jacket made him look bigger, more formidable than ever.

'Now put on this jacket,' he commanded, helping her into a leather jacket which was much too big for her.

'I feel ridiculous in it!' she protested, the cuffs coming down over her hands.

'It will be some protection for you though, supposing that we had a crash—not that that is likely; I'm a very experienced rider, but I'd be happier if you wore this,' he said, zipping it up, and standing so close that she was reminded of that moment on the beach when he had lain on top of her, naked, his body pressing her down. The memory sent heated blood rushing round her body; she couldn't look at him.

It was a deep relief when he helped her on to the pillion and swung in front of her. 'Hold on to my waist!' he ordered over his shoulder, and she tentatively slid her arms round him as he kick-started the powerful machine. His waist was slim, in spite of the leather jacket. Her fingers met on the other side.

A moment later they were riding up the stony private road to the public road running past the villa. It was only when they were out on the highway that Max let the throttle out and the motorbike really put on speed.

The ride was exhilarating. Olivia clung to Max's strong body, feeling as if they were moulded together, letting herself move with him, leaning this way and then that as he took the corners, the wind blowing her short hair up into golden filaments, her thighs forced against his, his blue jeans rubbing against her bare skin.

They drove past the lush olive groves which grew all over the island, past whitewashed houses set back from the road among orange and lemon trees, the dark tongues of cypress trees curling up against the blue sky. The air was full of the scent of flowers. The heat of the day was beginning to intensify now that the sun was riding higher in the sky, and Olivia felt perspiration trickling down her back, her thin yellow top sticking to her hot skin under the over-large leather jacket.

Corfu was a fascinating town, the architecture an international muddle of styles: a Byzantine church here, an elegant French ironwork balcony there, a Venetian subtlety down near the harbour, and elsewhere neo-classical Greek columns to be glimpsed beside plain modern villas. They even passed a flat green space where you could see English cricket being played, with men in white clothes running between the two wickets and people in straw hats sitting in deckchairs to watch, lazily clapping.

Corfu's history was complex; many races had come here over the centuries and left their mark behind them without making much impression on the Corfiots themselves, who continued to live as they always had, in the sun, growing their olives, looking after their sheep and goats on the herb-scented hills, where thyme and rosemary and basil grew wild, fishing in the rich blue sea, cooking in the tavernas and hotels, cheerfully accepting the tourists who flocked there.

As they rode down towards the harbour they passed a horse-drawn carriage slowly plodding along, under the fluttering awning a dreamy couple gazing out at the shops and tavernas they passed. The noise of Max's motorbike made the horse start in alarm, tossing its head, and plunging sideways across the road. The driver swore in Greek and reined his horse back tightly, soothing it with clicking tongue and murmured reassurance, then, as Max roared past, shouted angrily at him in Greek.

Max shouted back in the same language, grinning at him.

The driver waved a fist at him, but was laughing now.

'What did you say to him?' Olivia asked.

'You don't want to know!' Max turned his head to look at her, his dark eyes teasing. 'You must learn to speak Greek.'

'I am learning,' she said, then admitted, smiling, 'Slowly.'

'Well, I shouldn't learn what he just said!' Max said and laughed, slowing as they arrived down at the harbour.

His yacht was bigger than she had expected, and very impressive: white, sleek, fast and amazingly compact both in the two cabins and in the engine-room. It had been designed to be sailed by one person, but obviously it could hold several comfortably. It had sails too, which meant that Max could choose the form of power he preferred in whatever weather he found.

'She's wonderful,' Olivia said after the short tour of the vessel. 'I envy you. I've only got a dinghy.'

'Have you ever sailed around here?'

She shook her head.

'Would you like to?'

Her golden eyes glowed eagerly. 'I'd love to!'

He smiled at her, charm in the curl of his mouth. 'OK, give me a chance to check my radio, then we'll get under sail. There's enough wind today. Why don't you go and buy some food? Just bread, some cheese, a little salad—

tomatoes and onions, a lettuce—and some fruit for a dessert. We'll fish on our way, catch our lunch and cook it in the frying-pan. How does that sound?'

'Blissful,' she breathed, and his dark eyes glimmered.

'I can see you and I have the same tastes. Do you know Paki? Why don't we head that way? Have you been there?'

She turned her head out to sea, remembering the little islet which wasn't far from the coast of Corfu. 'Once, some years ago, by motorboat from the harbour here. I have a vague memory of a very green place, very peaceful.'

'When I was a boy we spent our holidays on Corfu— we had relatives here—and we always sailed over to Paki, every time we came. There are underwater caves there— fascinating places. If we have time I'll show you. I stayed on Paki for weeks a few years back, did nothing but catch lobsters and fish for mullet and snapper all day. When I wasn't fishing, I sunbathed and slept.'

'It sounds wonderful.' It sounded like the perfect holiday—she could imagine how it must have been. Paki was a tiny island covered in olive trees and vines and the maquis, that tangle of grass, herbs and spiky shrubs which in the sun gave out such an astounding scent, a scent which travelled for miles and met you long before you reached the island and which was the very essence of the Mediterranean coasts.

He watched her sensitive, revealing face intently, then said in a gentle voice, 'Off you go and do the shopping— have you got any money on you?'

She shook her head anxiously.

He laughed and produced some notes from a pocket in the leather jacket. 'This should be enough. Don't go too far, and don't be long. I won't take more than ten

minutes to check out my radio. Oh, yes...wait a
second...' He dived out of sight and came back a
moment later with a red string bag. 'Take this, you'll
need it.'

Olivia set off along the busy harbour, watching gulls
chasing their shadows across the blue sky, fishermen
mending nets or loading lobster-pots on to their boats,
behind her the rattle of mast wires, the flap of the wind
through sails, the slap of the water against the harbour
walls. She felt almost light-headed with happiness and
excitement. She couldn't wait to set out for Paki.

She had been here on Corfu for ten days and nothing
had happened until today—she had relaxed in the sun,
swum, eaten delicious Greek food, read one of the
paperbacks she had brought with her. She had barely
spoken to her father, or he to her; there had not, this
year, been any other visitors. Olivia had enjoyed herself,
but it had not been an exciting experience, merely a
peaceful one.

Since she met Max on the beach this morning everything had changed. She felt as if she had been asleep for
years, and suddenly woken up. She felt so alive. She
could almost feel the blood rushing round her body, the
air pumping in and out of her lungs...

She had never felt like this before; she was scared of
making too much of it. Max was probably only being
pleasant to the daughter of a man he was doing business
with; or maybe he was just bored and wanted someone
to help him pass the time. It couldn't mean more than
that. Not with a man like Max Agathios. And a girl like
her.

She made a rueful face. They were miles apart. Why
try to deny it? He was a lot older, for one thing, and,
for another...well, she wasn't naïve; he was far too at-

tractive not to have had a lot of other women, beautiful women, much more exciting women.

In fact, it was surprising he wasn't married.

She stopped in her tracks, standing still in the middle of the bustling street. What made her think he wasn't?

She hadn't thought about it before, but, now that she did, of course it was possible—no, probable—that he was married, a man of his age.

'Beautiful peaches,' a voice murmured coaxingly in English at her elbow and she started, realising only then that she had stopped right outside a greengrocer's shop.

She pulled a polite smile on to her face, answered in Greek, and saw the man's lined face break into surprised smiles.

A few minutes later she walked back to the boat with her net bag full of food and saw Max waiting for her on deck, the sun glittering on his raven-black hair, striking blue lights out of the thick strands of it. He had taken off his leather jacket, and the wind blew his T-shirt up and showed the tanned, flat planes of his stomach. Olivia felt her own stomach cramp in overwhelming attraction and her legs begin to tremble oddly.

She had to stop this happening! She mustn't lose her head over him. What did she know about him, after all?

He leaned on the polished wood rail and grinned down at her as she came aboard. 'Did you get everything?'

She held out the string bag, and his change. 'Yes. That was the first time I've ever shopped for food here—it was fun. I even managed to make myself understood in my pathetic Greek some of the time.'

He looked surprised. 'You do speak some Greek, then?'

'Anna teaches me while I'm here, and I have a tape I listen to every night while I'm here. Just tourist

phrases—please, thank you, where is the bank? That sort
of thing.'

'Well, good for you—very few visitors bother to learn
Greek, but it makes a big difference to us to have people
trying to speak our language instead of expecting us to
speak English.' He smiled, handing back the string bag.
'Will you put all this away in the galley and come back
up to help me? We'll leave at once. We can't be away
too long or your father might get worried.'

The galley was tiny and very compact—a place for
everything and everything in its place—the fittings all in
golden pine. Olivia put away the domed Greek bread,
the salad and fruit and cheese, then hurried back up on
deck to help Max set sail.

Minutes later they were moving out of the harbour
with a stiffish breeze filling the sails, the water creaming
past the sides of the boat. Max watched Olivia moving
around, nodding approval of her deft handling of the
ropes as they met the stronger waters of the sea outside
the harbour.

They took a couple of hours to sail to Paki, and
anchored off the coast just around eleven-thirty. Max
fished over the side, rapidly catching a small squid, which
he threw back, then some sardines, which he kept, and
a couple of red mullet.

They filleted the mullet, left the sardines whole, un-
filleted, then fried them all together, and served them
with salad, which Olivia had tossed together while Max
was fishing. She had squeezed a fresh lemon over the
contents of the wooden salad bowl and sliced the crusty
Greek bread, which smelt so good that her stomach
clenched in sudden hunger at the scent of it.

They ate their lunch on deck, the boat riding underneath them. The fish was better than anything Olivia

had ever eaten—she had never realised how good sardines could taste. There was almost nothing left for the screaming gulls which had gathered around at the smell of cooking fish.

After their white Greek cheese they turned their attention to the peaches Olivia had bought—big, yellow-fleshed, spurting with juice. Max made coffee in his battered old coffee-pot—not the usual Greek coffee, tiny cups of muddy black liquid syrup with sugar, but French coffee, served black, without sugar.

Olivia drank hers, then leaned back against the cushions propping her up and closed her eyes in the shadow of a canvas canopy Max had run out to give them some protection from the fierce afternoon sun.

'You aren't going to sleep, are you?' Max murmured, and she smiled lazily.

'Sounds wonderful to me.'

He laughed softly, his fingertip tracing the outline of her profile, his fleeting touch cool on her sun-flushed cheek.

'We shall have to sail back in an hour or so, or we'll find your father has raised an alarm for us. If you take a siesta, we won't have time to land on Paki.'

She yawned, hardly able to take in what he was saying. 'What?'

'I suppose we can always come back tomorrow,' he murmured. 'We could make an earlier start, get here by ten, land and eat ashore at one of the tavernas on Paki.'

Her lashes gold against her cheeks, Olivia dreamily said, 'That would be fun.'

She drifted off into blissful sleep and woke up with a start at the cry of a gull to find herself lying with her head on Max's shoulder, his arm around her.

As she shifted he looked down at her, their eyes very close; she saw the dark glaze of his pupils, tiny, almost imperceptible flecks of gold around them.

'Time to go back, I'm afraid,' he said, and she couldn't hold back a sigh of reluctance.

'I suppose we have to...'

'I don't want this afternoon to end either,' Max said softly and her heart turned over.

He slowly bent his head and Olivia lifted her own to meet his; their mouths touched, clung, in a slow, sweet, gentle kiss that set off a chain reaction through her whole body. Then she felt Max's hand slide up from her waist to her breast and gasped, quivering.

His mouth lifted; he looked at her, smiled. 'Am I going too fast for you? Don't worry, we'll take it at your pace, as slow as you like.' He paused, then said in an odd, wry voice, 'Olivia, am I crazy, or would I be...? No, not in this day and age, I don't believe it...'

Bewildered, she asked, 'What?' and he watched her in that strange, almost incredulous way.

'You're very lovely, you know that, Olivia—and I can't be the first man to notice the way you look, yet I get the feeling you haven't actually slept with anyone yet... Tell me I'm crazy! Not that it would make any difference, but you're so different from most girls I meet... So, are you?'

Very flushed now, she said, 'Yes... No... I mean... I haven't...' She was so embarrassed that she jumped and started brushing down her hair, pulling down her top. 'Shall we start back now?'

He got to his feet and started clearing the deck, a push of an electronic button sending the canopy back inside the top of the wheelhouse, the cushions all put away below. The anchor lifted, they set sail again, the breeze even stiffer now and blowing inshore so that they made good time back to Corfu.

While they sailed Olivia did the washing up and put things away in their accustomed places, relieved to be out of sight and out of his presence for a while. She was still getting over what he had said . . . the question he had asked. Had he really expected her to have slept with someone already? Admittedly, some girls she knew had already begun experimenting with boyfriends, but these days most people of her age were less likely to jump into bed at the first opportunity. AIDS had made that much of a difference.

They moored at Corfu harbour again, with the Judas trees which grew alongside casting their black afternoon shadows on them as they walked underneath to collect the motorbike from a nearby garage where Max had left it to be serviced while they were sailing.

They drove back to the villa as the heat of the day was dying down. Over his shoulder, Max shouted to her, 'I'm afraid we're quite late. I hope your father won't be too annoyed.'

Her arms holding on to him tightly because he was driving fast, Olivia said huskily, 'I hope not too.' Her father didn't normally mind what she did during the days she spent here; she wasn't thinking much about him and his reactions. She was more disturbed by the pleasure it gave her to feel Max's thighs against her bare inner legs, to press against his slim back, feel the motion of his body with hers as they swerved and swooped round corners with all the grace of a swallow in flight.

Ten minutes later they walked from the garage to the villa terrace, and met Gerald Faulton. Olivia's nerves jumped at the icy expression on his face.

'Where have you been?' he bit out, looking at her wind-blown hair and flushed face with distaste.

It was Max who replied. 'We left a message with your housekeeper—didn't you get it?'

Gerald Faulton turned his bleak eyes on Max. 'You've been gone since breakfast time. Do you know what time it is now?'

'I told Anna we might take my boat out—didn't she tell you that? We thought we would go over to Paki, fish, have lunch there. We've had a wonderful day.'

Her father did not look any happier. He stared at Olivia again, frowning. 'You have been on his boat with him all day?' he asked with ice on every syllable.

Max frowned too. 'I'm a good sailor, Gerald, I know what I'm doing. She was perfectly safe with me.'

'I sincerely hope she has been,' her father said through tight lips. 'I know some men find schoolgirls irresistible, but I didn't think you were one of them.'

Max stiffened, staring at him. 'Schoolgirls?' He repeated the word in a terse, hard intonation that made a shiver run down Olivia's back. He slowly turned his head to look down at her. 'What does he mean, schoolgirls? How old are you?'

All the colour had left her face. She had thought he knew. It hadn't occurred to her that he didn't. She hadn't pretended to be older than her age, she didn't wear make-up, she hadn't tried to fool him. Why was he looking at her like that? She couldn't get a word out.

'She was seventeen a couple of weeks ago,' Gerald Faulton told him. 'She has another year of school ahead of her, and I don't want her distracted before her final exams. I want her to do well enough to go on to university. I deliberately sent her to a single-sex school—I don't believe girls do as well if there are boys around. They are afraid to compete in case boys think they're blue-stockings.'

Olivia turned and ran into the villa, straight up the stairs to her bedroom. She knew there would be no trip to Paki tomorrow, no more rides on the back of Max's bike.

She didn't go down to dinner; Anna without comment brought her a crab salad on a tray an hour later, but she didn't eat any of it. She went to bed early and didn't sleep much.

She got up at dawn and went down to the beach as usual in the first primrose light of day, half hoping that Max might be there, half nervous in case he came. If they could talk, surely he would see—realise—that the years between them didn't matter that much. He had thought she was older, hadn't he? The essential person she was hadn't changed just because he now knew she was only seventeen. How old was he? she wondered, as she had wondered all night, during her waking hours of darkness. Late twenties? Thirty? Not much more than that.

OK, it was a big gap, but when she was twenty-five he would still be in his thirties, so it wasn't so terrible, was it? Men often married girls who were much younger than themselves. A lot of the businessmen who visited her father here brought much younger wives along with them.

If she could only talk to Max—but time passed, and he didn't show up; the beach was as empty as usual. She sunbathed and swam, sat staring out to sea feeling de-pressed. It would have been such fun to sail that beautiful white bird of a boat again today, to feel the sea swell under their feet and the wind in their hair, the maquis scent drifting out to meet them from Paki, to go diving maybe, when they arrived, and investigate the under-water caves. Olivia was a trained diver; she loved to explore the depths of the lake she lived beside, or the clear blue seas around Corfu.

She sighed, remembering the feel of Max's waist in her arms, the feel of his thighs pressing against hers as they rode along on the bike.

She should have known it couldn't be real—that exciting feeling in the pit of her stomach, the quiver of awareness every time he looked at her. She had been kidding herself. She was crazy.

Or was she?

Hadn't Max felt something too? He wouldn't have been so angry otherwise, would he, if he hadn't been attracted to her? She thought of the way his eyes had smiled at her, the way he had watched her on the beach early that morning, the way he had kissed her, his hands lingering as they touched her cheek, her throat, that soft brush of his fingers over her breast.

Colour crept up her face at the mere memory. She had been so deeply aware of him as a man, how could he not have been aware of her in the same way? Maybe she had imagined it. After all, she had never had a real boyfriend—only danced with boys at discos and had the odd kiss in a dark corner at a party. But could she have imagined everything that happened? The looks, the smiles, the tone of his deep, inviting voice?

Oh, what was the use of fooling herself? He had probably been nice to her for her father's sake! And now he knew that, far from pleasing her father, he had annoyed him, he would probably be distantly polite to her for the rest of his stay.

She walked back up to the villa and showered and changed for breakfast. As she was coming downstairs again she met her father, who gave her a hard, frowning glance.

'I want a word with you. Come into my study.'

Like a schoolgirl in front of the headmaster she stood while her father leaned against his desk, his arms folded. His gaze flicked down over her in that cold distaste he had shown when she returned with Max the previous day.

In a remote voice Gerald Faulton said, 'You should not have gone off all day with Max Agathios. You know that, don't you? It was reckless and foolhardy. You know nothing about the man.'

Flushed and upset, she burst out, 'We sailed to Paki, he caught some fish and we cooked it and ate it on board, then sailed back. Nothing else happened.' That wasn't the truth, the whole truth and nothing but the truth, but she wasn't telling him about the tenderness of that kiss, the brief brush of Max's hand on her breast. Her father wouldn't understand; he would leap to all the wrong conclusions.

'I'm relieved to hear it,' her father said, still distantly, then added in a dry voice, 'But he has something of a reputation with women. I might trust him as a business-man, but not with a woman, and he knew very well that he shouldn't take you out without getting my permission first.' Gerald's mouth twisted sardonically. 'Believe me, if he were your father, Max Agathios would never trust you with a man like himself!'

Red-cheeked, Olivia muttered, 'You're making too much fuss about nothing. In this day and age it is ridiculous...'

'I assure you, most Greek men would be just as pro-tective towards their young daughters. They wouldn't allow them to go off sailing alone, especially with someone like Max Agathios. They have more sense, and they understand their own sex. Left alone with an attractive woman, any man is tempted and, believe me, Max would never try this on with the daughter of one of his Greek friends.'

That wounded her. She knew it was true; she had far more freedom than many of the daughters of her father's local business friends. It hurt to think that Max had treated her with less respect than he would treat a Greek girl.

'What am I to do when I see him, then?' she asked miserably. 'Ignore him? After all, he is your guest...'

'Not any more,' her father said curtly. 'He has left and he won't be coming back.'

Olivia had been nerving herself to see Max again; she had sat on the beach and tried to work out what to say to him, how to thaw that hard, angry face back into human warmth. Now she felt as if a trapdoor had opened under her feet and she had dropped through into black, empty space.

He had gone, without even saying goodbye. She would probably never see him again.

Her father watched her pale face. 'And I shall have to be leaving tomorrow too, I'm afraid. Urgent business in Athens. There is no point in coming back either, my holiday is more or less over. So I've booked you on a flight tomorrow too, back to England.'

CHAPTER TWO

MONTHS later, Olivia discovered why Max Agathios had paid that sudden, unexpected visit to her father. One of her friends at school showed her a newspaper whose business pages carried a story about Max's shipping company.

'Your father sold this Greek guy some old ships, Loll, and now he's been made a director of the Greek company, it says here. And just look at the photo of the Greek guy!' Julie sighed noisily, gazing at the rather fuzzy picture of Max at the centre of the newsprint. 'If you ever meet him, tell him I think he's dead sexy.'

Olivia took the paper and sat down on the grass beside the tennis court on which they would shortly be playing. Julie turned her attention to the game in progress.

'Come on, you two! Speed it up! We're booked in here in five minutes!' she shouted at the girls playing, who yelled back rudely.

Olivia was reading the story with intent concentration. Julie had given her the gist of it succinctly enough: Max had bought two freight ships and a car ferry from her father earlier this year, the story ran, and now her father had been appointed to the board of directors of Agathios Kera, the shipping line operated by Max.

The story also told her something else—that Max and his brother Constantine had quite separate companies, and were in direct competition with each other, running ferries and freight ships between the Greek islands and mainland. The report claimed that both brothers had bid for Gerald Faulton's ships, and that Constantine, the older brother, was furious at being outbid by his younger brother. So that explained her father's phone call from Constantine! And Max's odd smile when he heard about it.

Olivia gazed at the picture of Max, her breathing quick. Julie was right. Even in the grey newsprint he looked sexy. Julie should see him in real life! Then her eye caught something she had missed in her first hurried reading of the story. Right there in the first sentence, immediately after Max's name, they had his age in brackets. Twenty-nine. She had been close enough in her guesswork then. He wasn't yet thirty.

She was now two months short of her eighteenth birthday, which made her just eleven years younger. It wasn't that big a gap, was it? she thought uncertainly, biting her lip.

Julie came back and flung herself down beside Olivia on the grass, her white skirts flaring, showing long, tanned legs. 'Are you going to stay at your father's Greek villa again this year?'

'I expect so,' Olivia said, mentally crossing her fingers.

Julie groaned. 'You might meet this Greek guy—lucky you! Can I come too?'

'Hands off,' Olivia said. 'He's mine.'

They both laughed, but secretly Olivia was serious. She felt sure she would see Max again that summer; it was a wild, irrational belief but a fixed one. She couldn't wait to get to Corfu.

A fortnight later she got a letter from her father telling her that he had sold his Corfu villa and was in the process of buying an apartment in Monaco. He suggested that this year they should stay at a hotel in the West Indies for their usual holiday together. She would probably find that more fun, he said; there would be plenty of young people of her own age around.

'The West Indies!' Julie said dreamily, reading the letter over Olivia's shoulder. 'I wish my dad would take me there, but he always goes back to Spain every year. As soon as I can afford to pay for my own holiday I am heading for the West Indies.'

Olivia wasn't really listening to her. She was staring at her father's immaculate handwriting, her golden eyes fixed and over-bright. She was saying goodbye to a dream. She had been living all year long on the hope that next summer there would be a re-run of the day she had spent with Max, and that this time there would be no abrupt ending, this time they would spend the whole summer together.

Now she knew it wasn't going to happen. She even had the feeling that her father had sold his villa to make sure it never happened. He might do business with him, sit on Max's board of directors, but she had picked up antagonism in him towards the younger man.

Olivia didn't know why her father felt that way, yet somehow she had felt it from the beginning. She had seen the coldness in his eyes whenever he looked at Max. Gerald Faulton did not like him. Why? she wondered, frowning. Was it just one of those indefinable dislikes, a mere clash of personalities?

Or was it because Max was twenty years younger, and already running his own company, being very successful? Business was all her father had ever really cared about—she could easily believe that he would resent a younger man coming along and successfully building up a business which might one day out-perform Gerald Faulton's company.

Of course, she could be imagining all this! Her father might have forgotten all about the day she spent with Max. He might have sold his villa for personal reasons of his own. No doubt he was buying a place in Monaco because it was a tax haven, whereas Corfu wasn't.

None of that mattered. All she cared about was that she wouldn't now be seeing Max.

Julie gave her a sideways look, her face curious. 'Why are you looking as if your pet rabbit just died? Don't you want to go to the West Indies?'

'Not much,' Olivia said truthfully.

In fact she didn't go anyway, because her mother had an accident the day before Olivia was due to leave. Another car pulled out of a crossroads, crashing into the side of Ann Faulton's car. When Olivia rushed to the hospital she found that her mother had serious injuries and would be kept in hospital for weeks, possibly months.

Olivia cabled her father the news, adding that she would not now be joining him in the West Indies. He sent her mother flowers and wrote to Olivia saying she was quite right to stay with her mother, and as soon as he had moved into his apartment in Monaco she must come to stay with him there.

Ann Faulton's recovery was slow and painful, even after she left hospital. Instead of going to college that autumn, Olivia stayed at home to nurse her mother. It was another six months before Ann Faulton was well enough to resume a normal life.

After that, Olivia took a part-time job working as a receptionist in the casualty department of the local hospital. Her mother didn't need her so much any more and

Olivia would have been bored doing nothing all day while she waited to start her course in public relations and media studies at college in the following autumn.

Ann Faulton was fully recovered, although her accident and the months of pain that followed it had aged her. She looked ten years older than she had, and she could no longer manage her job as a sports mistress. She retired, but she too hated having nothing to do, so after a few months she decided to open a sports shop in the Lake District.

Olivia had chosen a college two hours away from home so that she could visit her mother quite often. During her first year there, she lived on the campus, in a narrow little room as bare as a monk's cell, made a lot of new friends and learnt to live on very little, worked hard and went to a lot of parties.

She spent a fortnight with her father that summer in his elegant Monaco apartment with a view of the palace gardens, dark with cypress and brilliant with bougainvillaea. Gerald Faulton never mentioned either of the Agathios brothers, so eventually Olivia very casually asked over breakfast one day, 'Are you still on the board of Max Agathios's company?'

'Yes, why?' he asked, as if she might be an industrial spy, and she shrugged, still trying to look and sound totally offhand.

'You always say you want me to be interested in your business affairs. I read in the newspapers that you had joined the board of Agathios Kera, that's all...' She paused, then asked, 'Why Kera, by the way? What does that mean?'

'Leon Kera is a sleeping partner who put up some of the money for the company—he's a financier,' her father said flatly. 'The rumour is that Max Agathios is going to marry his daughter, which will keep the company in the family.'

Olivia's skin turned cold. 'Oh?' She took a painful breath. 'What's her name?' She had to know; she needed to know to believe it, to accept that Max was out of reach for her, that it was time to forget him.

'Daphne,' her father clipped out. 'She's Greek, a beautiful girl, typical Greek colouring—black hair, olive skin, dark eyes. She's clever too, a good head on her shoulders. She works with Max. I usually see her at board meetings, sitting beside him. More coffee?'

She shook her head, too stunned to speak, and her father got up from the table, putting his newspaper under his arm.

'Well, I have work to do,' he said, walking away without looking at her, to her relief, because she hated to think he might read her expression and guess at her feelings.

The last remnants of her dream had just died. She hadn't admitted it to herself, but she did now; for the past year she had gone on hoping that one day she would meet Max again and...

She broke off, biting down on her lower lip angrily. How stupid! She met a man once, spent a day with him, got kissed, and that was that. Why had she made such a big thing of it? He had probably forgotten her within a week.

Well, there were plenty of attractive guys around at her college. She had been keeping them all at a distance, turning down dates, refusing to get involved—but not any more. When she got back to college, she was going to have fun and forget Max Agathios.

* * *

The following two years were busy and enjoyable ones for Olivia. She did well in her course, and managed to get a good final result, and she was the centre of a lively social circle at her college. She went out with some of the best-looking men, but didn't fall in love with any of them, although several claimed they had fallen in love with her.

One guy asked her to live with him; another asked her to marry him. She turned them both down. Kindly. But firmly.

From time to time she read about Max in the newspapers. His company seemed to be growing rapidly—he was now running a cruise line around the Mediterranean and Aegean seas. She saw advertisements for his cruises all the time. He still seemed to run ferries in the Aegean, and had ships carrying freight from island to island there too, she gathered, but cruise ships were now the major part of his business.

From the sound of it, Max's company was now bigger than his brother's, or her father's. How did they like that? she wondered. They were both so competitive, and neither of them had much love for Max. It must be burning them up to see him forging ahead like this!

The summer of the year she left college she was invited to America for the whole summer by a guy she had been dating for months, but who was now returning for good to his Florida home after a year spent working in Britain.

His family had a beach house on the Keys in Florida; Gerry talked lovingly about brown pelicans and giant sea turtles, conch chowder and Key lime pie, mangrove swamps and glass-bottomed boats.

'I want you to meet my folks,' he said. 'And they're dying to meet you, they've heard so much about you.

Oh, come on, Loll—if you don't visit with us this year
we may never see each other again!'

Her mother persuaded her to join her father though.
After all, she pointed out, it was the only time they saw
each other during a year.

'OK, he isn't a loving father, but by his own rather
weird standards he's always tried to act like a father,
kept in touch, remembered your birthday and so on. I
think you should go.' Ann Faulton gave her a wry look.
'And from what you've told me about this Gerry, he's
getting far too serious about you, but you're not that
way about him. If you spend the summer with him and
his family he'll be entitled to think you like him more
than you do, Olivia.'

It was true, and, not for the first time, Olivia took
her mother's advice, told Gerry she was sorry but she
couldn't come to Florida, and went to Monaco instead.

The year since she last saw him showed her that her
father was beginning to show his age. Gerald Faulton
was now in his mid-fifties, and his hair was entirely silver,
his skin lined from years of sun-worshipping. His
regimen of diet and exercise had kept time at bay for a
long time, and he was still very slim and upright, but
Olivia felt a real pang of sadness as she realised that he
was beginning to lose the battle. His neck was wrinkling,
his jawline was no longer taut and firm, his eyes were
set deeper in his tanned skin and he no longer moved
with the same spring in his step.

His nature hadn't softened with time either; he was
as remote and cold of heart as ever. Within a couple of
days, Olivia was wondering why on earth she had taken
her mother's advice and come. Why did her father go
on inviting her when they had nothing in common,

nothing to talk about, and there wasn't a shred of warmth or affection between them?

At least the weather was good though; she could swim and sunbathe, and her father's small apartment was comfortable, indeed elegant.

One night Gerald suggested that they visit the Casino at Monte Carlo, the old Palais Casino on the main square, with its baroque décor, ornate, gilded, elegant. Olivia felt no excitement around the tables. She didn't want to play cards herself, or gamble on roulette; she soon grew bored with watching her father play baccarat, and instead began to wander around, looking at the *salles privées*, the silken brocade upholstery of chairs, the long swagged curtains, the paintings on the walls. She drank a glass of chilled white wine, a cup of coffee, nibbled nuts and crisps, watched over the bare white shoulders of a woman in black who was losing heavily at roulette, wondering how she could bear to throw her money away without a change of expression, and kept looking at her watch, hoping her father would show signs of getting bored.

Suddenly she realised that her father was no longer at the baccarat table.

He was standing near the main door of the big salon, talking to some people Olivia had never seen before— two men and a woman.

The older man was broad-set, wearing what she recognised as expensively tailored evening dress, his rather bull-like head set on heavy shoulders, his hair black, with a flash of silver at the temples. Olivia was not attracted by the ruthless force she read in his face and body, but she had read somewhere that power was an aphrodisiac, and she could believe it; some women might find him exciting.

Looking from him to the other, younger, man, Olivia saw such a strong likeness that it was obvious they were related; possibly brothers? No, the age gap was too great. They must be father and son.

The woman with them looked the right age to be the wife of the older man, yet she was so lovely Olivia found it hard to believe that she was the mother of a son in his twenties.

A slender, graceful woman with hair like black silk and eyes like jet, she wore a white dress that was elegant and yet sensual, clinging to her body from her shoulders to her ankles, covering everything and yet hinting at what lay underneath so that every man who passed her turned to stare as if wondering exactly what she was hiding.

Olivia watched her smiling sleepily, sensually, at Gerald Faulton, saw the way her father looked back, not even trying to hide the fact that he coveted the wife of another man, and was startled. She hadn't seen her father look that way at any woman before. It was not in his rather chilly nature, not in his controlled temperament.

But there was no doubt about it. Her father had an almost tranced look on his face, a flush on his high cheekbones, a brightness in his eyes.

Quickly, Olivia looked at the man she had decided must be this woman's husband. How did he feel about the way her father was watching his wife?

Or was she his wife?

Oh, yes, she thought, seeing a glitter in the man's heavy-lidded eyes, a streak of angry red staining his cheeks. That was a possessive, angry look, the instinctive reaction of a man watching his wife with someone else, and then something odd happened—he deliberately lowered his rather heavy lids, veiling that expression, as if he didn't want Gerald to see it.

Olivia was struck by that. Why was he afraid to let her father see his angry reaction?

Who was he? Someone who worked for her father? Someone who wanted to do business with her father?

It was very odd; she felt a distinct sense of familiarity whenever she looked at him. Had they met before, after all? She didn't remember it. And yet there was something...

While she was struggling to pin down whatever memory was trying to surface, her father turned to stare in her direction, and all the others looked round too.

Gerald Faulton made a peremptory gesture, beckoning her.

Olivia sighed, but obeyed, walking across the hushed, crowded room towards them, edgily aware of being watched all the way.

She was wearing her only really good evening dress, a classic backless slipper satin, tawny-coloured, with a deep V-neck, which left her shoulders and arms bare, the long skirts clinging from her waist to her thighs and then flowing easily down to her feet. The colour gave depth and brightness to her blonde hair, matched the golden colour of her eyes.

Her father had bought it for her, after deciding that nothing Olivia had brought with her was good enough for a party they had been to the night after she arrived.

The lifestyle on Corfu had been very different—far more casual and relaxed, a real beach holiday in the sun with a party style to match. Here, Gerald Faulton moved in circles who loved any excuse for dressing up: putting on jewellery, clouds of perfume, expensive designer dresses, the women competing to look the most stunning, the men apparently wanting the best-looking woman on their arm each night.

Gerald had gone with Olivia to choose the dress. It was ready-made, but designed by a top French couturier, and luckily fitted her as if it had been made for her, but Olivia wasn't quite comfortable in it—it was so formal, and yet left so much of her bare.

'Ah, there you are, Olivia. I want you meet some friends of mine... You've heard me mention Constantine Agathios, haven't you?'

She stiffened, her hand already held out, her eyes on the man's heavy, olive-skinned face.

It was a shock, and yet it wasn't. No wonder he had looked familiar! No wonder she had been increasingly sure she had seen him somewhere before.

He and Max might only be half-brothers, but they shared a family resemblance which was very marked, in spite of the age gap between them. She should have guessed at once. She was sure she would have guessed, sooner or later, if she hadn't been told.

He took her hand and Olivia shivered involuntarily as those large, tanned fingers swallowed hers up. She almost wondered if he would let her hand go again; did he ever let anything go? Meeting those heavy-lidded eyes was even more unnerving. This was a difficult, complicated man, she thought, staring back at him.

There was something belligerent, choleric, in that face; he had a temper, from the look of him. Not an easy man to deal with, or maybe even like? A bull on the point of charging, she thought—that was the impression he left on her, and yet there was something else, a craftiness about the half-hidden eyes, the line of the selfish mouth. She remembered the angry glitter of his eyes when her father stared covetously at his wife, the way Constantine Agathios had swiftly veiled that look, hiding it away. This man was full of rage, but he was cunning enough to hide it, which made him disturbing.

'I am delighted to meet you, Olivia—may I call you Olivia? You are very like your father. I feel I know you already, and you must be the same age as my son here, Christos,' Constantine said, and smiled suddenly, full of charm which Olivia didn't quite trust, although she blinked in surprise as it focused on her. That was something else he had in common with Max—Max had that charm, too, only in him it was genuine, full of warmth. She was sure that Constantine's charm was skin-deep.

'Thank you,' she murmured, flickering a look at the younger man. So she had been right—it was his son!

'What a beautiful dress—that colour is perfect with your wonderful English complexion and hair,' said the woman beside Constantine, in a deeply accented voice.

'My wife, Helena,' Constantine introduced her, letting go of Olivia's hand at last so that she could shake hands with his wife, who smiled in that languid, sleepy way at Olivia, as she had at Gerald.

'I always envy English women. They don't have the problem of coping with too much sun, ruining their skins, giving them wrinkles and lines before they're middle-aged. In my country, the sun is a woman's enemy.'

'We just have to cope with rain,' Olivia said, smiling back.

'You English always complain about your weather, but rain is so good for the skin that I only wish it rained in Greece every day!'

'If it did, you wouldn't,' Olivia drily said, adding, 'Anyway, your skin is wonderful—I wish I had that tan!'

'Thank you.' Helena smiled, accepting the compliment gracefully, a woman used to compliments yet silently immune to them, Olivia felt. Not vain, simply knowing precisely how she looked.

With that skin which had the polished lustre of gold silk, a light tan overlaying the original olive complexion, very few lines around her mouth and eyes, she could have been any age from thirty to fifty.

'My mother never sunbathes,' said the young man beside Helena. 'She wears a hat whenever she goes out in the sun, and lots of sunblock, yet she always seems to have her tan! I think it is just the natural colour of her skin.'

Olivia looked at him and felt her heart skip a beat, because Christos Agathios looked the way she was sure Max must have done at that age.

His black hair was very curly, whereas Max's hair was straight, and his face wasn't so tough, so honed and taut, but the family likeness was unmistakable, and so was the family charm which shone out of his smile, in this case a charm which held warmth and light-hearted humour.

'I've heard a lot about you,' he said, and her eyes widened.

'Who from?' she asked, faintly breathless. Max? Had Max talked about her?

Christos laughed. 'Your father, of course! Who else?'

Disappointment seeped through her, but she managed a pretence of laughter. 'Of course, silly question.' Why on earth would Max have mentioned her to his nephew, anyway?

Christos looked past her into the glitter of the salon, the fixity of the gamblers around the table, the tension in the air. He made a face, his nose wrinkling.

'Dead boring, isn't it? Why don't we go on some-where a bit livelier? I know a great nightclub not far from here—we can dance to some terrific music and you can meet some of my friends. They're all going to be there tonight.'

Her eyes brightened. 'I'd love that.' Then she looked at her father, her smile fading. She could never remember her father going to a nightclub or anywhere like that; he didn't like noisy pop music and he wasn't a big nightclub fan. She couldn't see him agreeing to Christos's suggestion.

He did though, immediately, all smiles. 'Good idea, why don't we make a night of it?'

On the way, she asked Christos, 'Have your family got an apartment here too?' and he shook his head.

'We borrowed one from a friend for a month. Your father said you just left college—have you got a job set up?'

'Yes, in London, in the marketing and public relations department of my father's company. What do you do?'

'Work with my father too.'

They grinned at each other. 'Nepotism for both of us, then,' Olivia said, and they laughed.

'I'm in the accounts department at the moment,' Christos confided. 'I did an economics degree in the States. But I'll take over running the firm one day so I'll move around from one office to the other until I know how the whole operation works.'

'That seems a good idea. I hope I'll be doing something like that, although economics isn't my strong point.' She grimaced and Christos laughed.

'Nobody can be good at everything. I expect your father has enough accountants working for him, anyway. He only has one daughter.'

'Yes,' Olivia said, not for the first time wondering how her father really felt about that. He must have hoped for sons to inherit the firm. Did he resent the fact that she hadn't been a boy? Did that explain the coldness in his eyes whenever he looked at her?

The nightclub was ultra-modern, with a rainbow of laser lights criss-crossing the darkness and the very latest music played continuously. The DJ was lively, professional, speaking English and French alternately, both very fluently, telling jokes in both, playing music from both countries. The floor was underlit with a cloudy light which shone upwards, giving a glimmer to faces as people danced.

At some stage her father, Constantine and Helena all slipped away, but Olivia hardly noticed them leaving. Christos had introduced her to a crowd of young people he had met down there. They were an international lot—English, French, some Greek—lively and friendly, easy to get on with. They all sat around on leather couches, talking and laughing, drinking, eating the only food the club offered—faintly stale *sandwich au jambon*: chunks of dry French bread with thin slices of ham between them.

She danced with a few guys, but mostly with Christos, and time slid by without Olivia ever even looking at her watch.

She was stunned, when they left eventually, to realise that dawn was breaking. Where on earth had the night gone?

Christos stopped in the strangely still and silent main square, empty for once of traffic, the shutters up over every window, Monte Carlo sleeping all around them.

Looking down at her with bright, sleepless eyes, he said, 'I don't want to go home yet, do you? Let's eat breakfast at a terrace café. I know somewhere that does a great croissant and the best coffee you can drink.'

She didn't want the night to end either. They ran, with linked hands, like children, through the streets, getting attentive looks from one of Monaco's policemen because they were still in evening dress and laughing, and might be drunk and a possible problem. Monaco had more policemen to the square inch than anywhere else in the world; that was why so many very rich people lived there. They felt safe and protected.

Olivia and Christos sat at a table outside on the pavement for an hour, drinking strong coffee, eating crisp, flaky croissants, watching the sun rise and the traffic around them thicken as the rest of the world woke up and set off to work.

They were still laughing, talking about films and favourite pop stars and what they liked to read. Christos had a terrific sense of humour; he was funny, quick with his retorts, kept her giggling.

Reluctantly, she looked at her watch at last and said, 'I suppose I'd better get home before my father calls the police.'

Christos grinned. 'And I bet he would too. Your father scares the living daylights out of me!'

She knew he didn't mean it. Christos wasn't the easily scared type. Life didn't hold much that scared Christos; he had too much of his father's nature in him. He might laugh a lot, but there was bedrock somewhere, under his friendly charm.

'What shall we do tonight?' he asked. He was taking it for granted that she would see him again, but Olivia wasn't offended. She didn't pretend she had another date, just laughed at him.

'You're sure of yourself, aren't you!'

He smiled into her eyes. 'We had fun last night, didn't we? And we both want to go on having fun. I've got a car. Why don't we drive to Juan-les-Pins, have dinner, then cruise the cafés—go to the Pam-Pam, Le Crystal, Le Refuge? Juan-les-Pins is always good fun, isn't it? If you sit in the Pam-Pam long enough you see everyone you know sooner or later.'

'Everyone *you* know, maybe! My friends never go there. Nor do I. Never been there in my life.'

'I'm shocked. Then we certainly must go tonight. You'll love it. It's crazy and as brassy as a fairground, but never dull.'

'Sounds like you, then!' mocked Olivia, and he roared with laughter.

When she got back to the apartment on Boulevard St-Paul, Olivia was nervous as she quietly unlocked the front door. She hoped her father would be asleep, then he might never realise that she had been out all night.

She was in luck. The apartment was silent, the door of her father's room closed. Olivia tiptoed into her own bedroom, undressed, washed, and went to bed. She was asleep almost before her head touched the pillow.

When she woke up it was afternoon; the room was shadowy because she had not opened the shutters but through the slats she could see sunlight gleaming. She looked at the clock and got a shock when she saw that it was nearly three. In the afternoon, she realised, and for a moment couldn't understand why she was in bed at that hour of the day. Was she ill?

Then she remembered, and almost fell out of bed. What on earth would her father say? When she'd showered, she nerved herself, opened her bedroom door, went in search of him, only to discover that the apartment was empty. He must have gone out.

He got back an hour later and never asked Olivia a single question, but simply told her he had had a phone call from a friend, inviting him to dinner—did she want to come along? It was an informal meal, it wouldn't matter if she didn't want to go.

'Well, Christos did ask me out...' she began, and her father looked pleased.

'Fine, then I'll go alone tonight. I'm glad you like Christos—you'll enjoy your visit more, having young people to go around with.'

Olivia loved Juan-les-Pins from the first moment she saw it. They left quite early, to drive from Monaco along the Corniche to Nice, then along the motorway to Antibes, across Cap d'Antibes, the promontory which thrust out into the sea, an expensive and exclusive part of this coast, covered in gardens and trees, with narrow roads going up and down the hill in a criss-cross pattern. Hidden behind high walls and large gardens lay the whitewashed villas of the very rich, sleeping in the sun. The top of the hill was surmounted by an old lighthouse; from up there visitors could view the surrounding landscape, Christos told Olivia when they too stopped there in the warm evening light and had a Coke under the plane trees.

'There's Juan-les-Pins, down there,' he said, gesturing.

As they drove off the Cap, Olivia realised how Juan-les-Pins had got its name—there were not many pines left, but you could imagine how pretty it must have been when there had been little here but pine trees and sand. There were still some pines around the Casino area, but everywhere else had been built on; the blocks of apart-

ments and hotels and cafés were so close together that
it was a bottleneck of traffic by day, but at night it glittered with lights and throbbed with pop music.

The tiny, winding streets were thick with traffic, the
pavements crowded with tourists out to have a good time,
the cafés and bars pounding with music and laughter
and people talking.

Olivia and Christos met some of the people they had
seen at the nightclub the night before, and she soon
realised that that was no coincidence—Christos had
known they would be in Juan-les- Pins. The group visited
a different resort every night, drifting around from one
bar to another, dancing, talking, drinking coffee or wine,
watching everyone else walking past on the pavements.

They did not get back to Monaco until the early hours
again, but now Olivia knew that her father wouldn't say
a word, even raise an eyebrow. He was delighted that
she was dating Christos.

For the next couple of weeks that was the pattern of
their days and nights. Olivia slept every morning and
spent the afternoon swimming and sunbathing, and in
the evening Christos arrived to take her out. Looking
back on these days, it all seemed to be a shimmer of
sunlight and laughter, a heady sense of freedom now
that her exams were over and she had not yet begun to
work for her living. Christos was the perfect playmate—
she enjoyed being with him, and she liked him more than
anyone else she had ever dated.

She only wished these days didn't have to end. If only
real life need never break in on them! That was how she
felt about this holiday—that it wasn't quite real, a golden
fantasy of sun and sea and glittering evenings together.
She would miss Christos when they left here. She wished

he lived in London and they could meet again—or wouldn't their relationship work back in grey, rainy, all too real old London?

It never entered her head that Christos might ask her to marry him.

Two days before she was due to leave Monaco Olivia was just about to walk into the sitting-room when she overheard her father talking on the phone. 'Kera died last night,' he said in a curt, clipped tone. 'I just got a call from Opie. As soon as the funeral is over... The next board meeting...'

Olivia halted, her hand on the door. Was he talking to Max? She was angry with herself for the immediate prickle of her nerves, the heat hitting her skin. What if he was? So what? Don't be so stupid! she told herself.

She heard her father hang up, heard the window on to the balcony being slid open. Olivia took a deep breath, walked in there, saw Gerald standing in the sunshine, staring down over the pink palace of the Grimaldi family, the hereditary princes of Monaco, but from his heavy frown, his abstracted air, not even seeing the beauty of the view.

As she walked out to join him he started and gave her a blank look. 'Oh, Olivia! There you are. Yes. I was just on the phone to Constantine...'

'Constantine?' she repeated, taken aback. Was he lying? But why on earth should he?

'Yes. I've invited him and Helena, and Christos, to dinner for your last evening here.' He pulled his wallet out of his inner jacket pocket, counted out some bank-notes, handed them to her. 'I want you to look pretty for the occasion. Buy something new, something very special.'

Dazedly, she took the money, not really listening, her mind on Max. Was her father going to tell her that Max's partner had died? Had Max married Daphne Kera yet? And who on earth was Opie?

She could hardly ask her father. She knew she would only get that cold, remote stare, and be snubbed for her pains. Gerald had always been secretive.

Whenever Gerald had a dinner party he brought in a professional chef with his own staff so that neither he nor Olivia had to worry about the arrangements for the evening. They could concentrate on their guests.

The party went as smoothly as they always did, yet Olivia sensed tension in the room all evening. Her father and Constantine were in an odd mood: excited yet edgy. Helena was very quiet; she hardly said a word, watching her husband with what seemed to Olivia to be anxiety. Even Christos was not himself. He drank several glasses of wine with dinner, then went on to have a double brandy at the coffee stage, which made Constantine scowl at him.

'You've had enough to drink!'

Olivia saw Helena put her soft, tanned hand on her husband's dark sleeve, saw him turn his bull-like head to glare down at her. She didn't say anything, but her eyes must have pleaded, because he made a rumbling noise in his throat and fell silent.

'Christos, why don't you and Olivia get some fresh air, out on the balcony?' Gerald calmly suggested.

They stood together in the shadows of the balcony, looking at the glitter of Monte Carlo's lights around and below them. Far out to sea they could see a large boat moored, lit up like a Christmas tree, so that they could even see the people on deck dancing and standing about with drinks in their hands.

'One day I'm going to have a big yacht of my own,' said Christos, with a sort of desperate belligerence.

'Don't forget to invite me along on your cruises!' Olivia joked, and he turned to her suddenly, his face flushed, his breathing audible.

'If you married me, you'd always come along!' And then, before she quite took in what he'd said, he went on in a rush, 'Let's do it...let's get married, Olivia.'

She stared blankly for a second. 'Is this one of your jokes?' she asked, ready to laugh, but saw in disbelief that he wasn't being funny.

'Of course it isn't! Would I make a joke about something like that?' He sounded upset; he certainly wasn't laughing. There wasn't a flicker of humour in his eyes. He looked so serious, unsmiling, his voice husky, his face dark red.

She stared at him, too stunned to know what to say.

Christos grabbed her hand, lifted it to his mouth, kissed the palm, whispering, 'Please, Olivia...say yes...say you'll marry me... You've got to marry me...'

Nobody had ever looked at her with such helpless pleading eyes, sounded so much as if they really needed her. All Olivia's female instincts made her weak, warmth and compassion softening her.

'Oh...Christos...' she began in a quivering voice. She couldn't remember afterwards what she actually said, but it must have added up to yes, because Christos kissed her with such vehemence that she almost suffocated, then, holding her hand tightly, he pulled her back in to the sitting-room where the others were talking and drinking coffee, and burst out excitedly, 'Olivia and I are engaged!'

For one second there was a silence and Olivia saw the faces of Constantine and her father turned towards her.

They each had an identical expression—she didn't have time to be certain what it was before they were on their feet, smiling, exclaiming, kissing her cheek, shaking Christos by the hand.

Helena kissed her too, but seemed almost as surprised and taken aback as Olivia herself felt.

'Darling, Olivia is a lovely girl. I hope you're going to be really happy,' Helena told her son, hugging him, but her eyes were worried, and Olivia didn't blame her for looking so uncertain. Olivia was uncertain herself.

Gerald produced chilled champagne and fluted crystal glasses, they drank a toast, and Olivia looked up at Christos and couldn't help wondering if she was imagining all this. It had happened out of the blue; she hadn't expected it.

Engaged. She was engaged. She was going to marry Christos. She still couldn't believe it. But one thing was certain—her father and Constantine Agathios were very happy indeed, and Christos was euphoric, talking in an almost light-headed way, laughing at nothing, drinking far too much champagne.

Olivia watched him with warmth, smiling whenever their eyes met. It touched her that he should have been so nervous about proposing to her. He was a darling. No doubt about that. She did love him. She really did.

So why did she feel panic rising inside her every time she thought about marrying him?

CHAPTER THREE

'BUT you've only known him for a few weeks!' her mother said, stunned by the news which Olivia told her when she got back from Monaco on the following evening.

'That's why we've agreed to wait until next summer for the wedding. Oh, Mum, don't you think we realise we have a lot to learn about each other? We're not daft enough to rush into marriage yet.'

Olivia herself was still faintly bemused, couldn't quite believe it. Christos had driven her to Nice airport to catch her plane home that morning, and they had talked soberly in the car, and in the noisy terminal before she went through the departure gate.

Suddenly everything had seemed different. She was going back to real life, a raincoat over her arm because she knew it was raining in London and she would need it when she arrived there. The holiday was ending, the gaiety of beach life already receding into memory.

Except that she and Christos were engaged and she was wearing a ring he had given her that morning, a large sapphire set in a ring of diamonds, which they had stopped off in Nice to buy before driving to the airport. Olivia hadn't wanted a ring, had protested that it could wait—why didn't they buy one later? But Christos had insisted so fiercely that she had given way, especially as he had told her that it was his father who was paying for the ring. It was his engagement present to them.

Her mother looked at it now as it flashed on Olivia's finger, frowning. 'Your father didn't push you into this, did he? I mean, I can see he would be thrilled to get you married off to someone with such good shipping connections, but don't let him talk you into anything you don't want to do, Olivia.'

Olivia sighed. She didn't pretend not to understand what her mother was saying.

'I think Father did sort of... Well, he and Christos's father, Constantine Agathios, hoped... Oh, there was a touch of matchmaking going on!' She was sure about that now. She and Christos had been thrown together deliberately in the hope that they would be attracted to each other.

Ann Faulton looked angry. 'I don't like this, Olivia, I don't like the sound of it at all.'

'They can't force me to marry Christos if I don't want to, Mum, don't worry, and I don't believe they can make Christos do anything he doesn't want to do either. He's far too independent. Wait until you meet Christos—you'll like him, I know you will.'

Ann Faulton walked round the little sitting-room of her Lake District home, bristling like an angry cat. If she had had a tail, it would have been twitching from side to side.

'He was always cold-blooded and hard-headed, but I didn't think even Gerald would try to sell you off as part of a business deal! That's what he's up to, isn't it, he and Agathios?'

'I don't honestly know what they're up to, but at least Christos agreed with me that we should wait until next year; he thinks we need to get to know each other better too.' Olivia paused, choosing her words carefully. 'I don't think Christos is all that sure either. Oh, he likes me.

And it's mutual. Really, Mum, he's a darling, but I just don't know yet if it would work out between us. And anyway, we're both going to be busy for a while. I start work in the London office on Monday, and Christos is coming to London too, in November. At the moment he's working in Greece, but his father apparently plans to take over some new offices in the City, in St Mary Axe, which isn't far from where I'll be, so we'll be able to meet often once Christos arrives, and until then we're going to write to each other, and talk on the phone.'

Ann Faulton sighed. 'Well, as soon as Christos arrives you must bring him up here for a weekend, so that I can find out for myself what he's like.'

'I will, don't worry,' promised Olivia.

At the weekend she and her mother piled everything they could manage into the back of Ann Faulton's roomy estate car and drove down to London, so that Olivia could move into her new home, a one-room studio flat on the first floor of an Edwardian house in Gospel Oak, a northern suburb close to Camden Town.

Her mother drove back next day, and Olivia spent that Sunday arranging and rearranging her new territory, her stomach cramped with nerves whenever she thought of starting work in the morning.

The offices of Grey-Faulton were familiar to her, of course; she had often visited them in the past but only briefly, to meet her father before joining him for lunch nearby in his favourite restaurant, a lofty, gloomy room above an old public house a stone's throw from Liverpool Street Station.

The London office was not as large, or as busy, as the Aberdeen office, which had taken on new importance with the discovery of oil in the North Sea, requiring

marine servicing of the oil-rigs, the delivery of freight
to them, and the hire of merchant vessels by oil
companies for a number of purposes. Gerald Faulton
was more likely to be in Scotland than London for most
of the year, since the bulk of the company business was
done north of the border, but he kept a small London
office because a portion of his trade was still done in
the south.

Olivia's job would cover all aspects of the company's
business. Once she had settled into the daily office
routine, her father wanted her to travel, as he did, meet
their employees at the various ports from which they
operated, get to know as much as possible about what
the firm did.

Pale and tense, she walked along St Mary Axe and
into the narrow entrance of the building on that Monday
morning. It was dead on the stroke of nine when she
arrived; it was raining, a grey, drizzly rain, which made
the roof tiles look black, dripped down the back of
Olivia's neck and depressed her spirits even further.

In the reception lobby she found the chief clerk
waiting, neat and grey-haired, with a clipped moustache
and the air of a fussy terrier shepherding a lost lamb.

'Miss Faulton, welcome, punctual to the second, just
like your father, and your grandfather before him,' he
barked cheerfully, bustling forward to shake hands as
soon as he saw her. 'Nowadays nobody bothers about
a thing like that, but in my young days they taught us
that punctuality was the courtesy of kings, and the men
of your family never forgot that.'

'Hello, Mr Robner, thank you,' she managed, feeling the covert stares of the two girls working behind
the counter.

They were there to deal with anyone who walked in off the street—the public wanting information or advice or someone calling to see an executive in the offices, or a crew member calling to see the personnel department.

Olivia wished that Mr Robner hadn't felt it necessary to come down to the front office to meet her on her first morning. She would rather have slipped in anonymously. She wanted to make friends with everyone who worked there, not put their backs up. Now they would all suppose that she expected to be treated like a princess, when what she really wanted was to be an ordinary member of the staff.

'Come along and I'll show you your office,' Mr Robner told her, guiding her towards the lift.

She followed him, sighing.

She spent the rest of the day alone in her recently redecorated office, waiting for the phone to ring, or someone to come in to see her. She sat at her desk and read the day's newspapers, shipping trade magazines, brochures. She watched the fax machine rattling out messages which never seemed to require answering, and didn't really apply to her. She read the letters on the most recent file, then ran out of things to do and stood by the window, listening to the rain splashing in the gutters, stared down into the street, watching people walk along the opposite pavement under bobbing umbrellas.

It was a relief to escape for an hour, for lunch. She ate a sandwich and did some shopping. Feeling slightly better, she tried a smile on the girls in the front office when she came back, and got blank, frosty looks in reply. It was a ghastly day. Olivia felt like running home. She felt like resigning there and then.

Back in her flat she sat down with a cup of strong black coffee, on the point of tears. It was all going to

be so dreary, day after day of rain and hostile looks from
the others who worked in the office. They hated her. She
should never have taken this job.

The phone rang. She almost jumped out of her skin.
She leaned over to pick it up. 'Hello?'

'Olivia?' a warm, confident, familiar voice said, and
at once her heart lifted.

'Christos!' Her eyes brightened. 'Oh, Christos, thanks
for ringing. I was dying to talk to you! Where are you?'

'London,' he said, and she took a surprised breath.

'But I thought you were going straight back to Greece!'

'Something urgent came up.'

She picked up an odd note in his voice and frowned.
'Is something wrong?'

'Nothing for you to bother about,' Christos said hurriedly. 'Just business. We're here for a couple of days—
how about dinner tonight?'

'I'd love it,' she said.

'Pick you up in half an hour.'

She had to rush to get ready in time. She put on a
dark brown and cream silk tunic, did her hair and face,
used a perfume she had brought back from France.
Christos arrived just as she was inspecting her reflection; he had come in a taxi which waited while he
rang her doorbell.

She opened the door and for a second they were both
unsure, surprised by the sight of each other in those un-
familiar surroundings, then Christos gave her his warm,
loving smile and kissed her mouth, and she was so glad
to see a smiling face that she clung, kissing him back
eagerly. He lifted his head and she saw his eyes; she knew
she had never kissed him quite that way before. He was
startled. Was he even taken aback? Or was she imagining things?

He didn't say anything, just put an arm around her and ran her back to the taxi.

'So how was your first day at work?' he asked, as they drove off through the rain.

It was a safe, neutral subject and the atmosphere between them was not yet as casual and easy as it had been in Monaco until he proposed, so she plunged into talk about her job. 'Oh, it was ghastly, Christos. I didn't do a thing, there was simply nothing to do, I was so bored all day. The phone didn't ring, nobody came to see me except the chief clerk, and he was horribly obsequious because he's scared stiff of my father. I think I'm going to hate this job! It is going to be so dull.'

'Wait until there's a disaster... a ship goes down or there's an accident, a man is killed or a hold catches fire...' Christos said soberly. 'I haven't worked in PR but I know one thing—something is always happening on ships, something is always going wrong. Especially on merchant ships. Cargoes can be damn tricky. And when things go wrong the shipping company is always to blame. That's when the phone will ring and you'll be busy all day talking to the Press and trying to minimise the damage to the company. You'll wish for some peace and quiet then.'

'Is it really that bad?' she asked, surprised by his vehemence.

'It can be. We have a PR department which is kept pretty busy with one project or another, when it isn't fielding Press questions or thinking up ways of protecting our image. These days we're always being accused of discharging oil and causing environmental disasters, and it isn't some lazy, thoughtless fool of a sailor who gets the blame, it's the company who pays his salary, even if the company has a strict rule to cover discharge of oil.'

Olivia grimaced. 'Well, I must admit I feel pretty strongly about that too. Have you ever seen a seabird trying to fly with wings that are soaked in black crude oil? It's heart-rending. I just hope I never have to deal with that situation—I might not be very good at defending the company if we've caused that sort of nightmare.'

The taxi slowed and pulled up outside the hotel in Mayfair where Christos and his father were staying. Christos paid the driver, the hotel porter came out with an umbrella and they got in out of the rain and went straight in to dinner.

'Where is your father tonight?' she asked over their first course, a rich, creamy chicken soup which was just right for such a wet, cold evening.

'Oh, I don't know, he never tells me anything,' Christos said, making a face. 'Don't let's talk about him. Tell me what your mother said when she heard about us.'

She didn't tell him about her mother's suspicions. Did he guess at them anyway? 'She wants to meet you as soon as possible. When can you come up to the Lake District for a weekend?'

His expression was wry. 'I'll ask my father. I think we're going back to Greece on Wednesday or Thursday, but he might let me stay on to visit your mother. Especially if you ask him—he'll do it for you. He wants you to be happy.'

She laughed disbelievingly. 'Who are you trying to kid? I don't believe he cares whether I'm happy or not.'

Christos gave her an odd look that held either irony or cynicism. 'You're wrong. At the moment it's all he cares about.'

Olivia stared at him, wondering if she was imagining that look in his face, the dry tone of his voice, but at that second out of the corner of her eye she caught sight of someone walking rapidly through the lobby of the hotel, which she could see reflected in the mirrors on the wall of the dining-room.

'There's my father!' she exclaimed. 'I thought he was still in Monaco! What's he doing here? Maybe I'd better run after him and tell him I'm here?'

Christos caught hold of her wrist as she rose. 'No, don't. He is here to see my father. On urgent business.'

Olivia sat down again, and he let go of her.

'Business at this time of night?' she asked, and he shrugged.

'You know them. Day or night, business comes first with them. I told you, we're in London on urgent business.'

'And my father is involved in it somehow? I didn't realise he did any business with your father.'

Christos had that cynical look again. 'They're old friends. They've done plenty of deals in the past.'

'Is my father on your board, as well as on the board of your uncle's company?'

Christos grinned, amused. 'Of course not. Uncle Max wouldn't like that idea at all!'

A shiver ran down Olivia's back. She must have caught a chill, she thought.

'Don't you know anything about your father's business?' asked Christos, staring at her in that odd way, his mouth twisting.

'Not much, but I suppose I'll learn a lot more now I work there,' she said as the waiter brought their second course. She had chosen piperade, a Basque dish of peppers, tomatoes and onions, cooked until they were almost a purée, when eggs were added and scrambled into the vegetable mixture. It was light and delicious. Christos had a steak, very rare, with salad.

They finished their meal with coffee and then Christos wanted to go on to a nightclub, as they had in the South of France every night, but Olivia regretfully had to point out that she must get up in the morning and go to work.

'I'm a wage slave now, I'm not on holiday!' she said, and he pulled a face at her.

'How boring.' But he amicably took her home in another taxi at eleven o'clock and kissed her goodnight at her front door before leaving.

'How about dinner tomorrow? I'll pick you up here at seven.'

In bed that night she lay awake for a while thinking about Christos, wondering if he was really in love with her. Even more puzzling, was she really in love with him? When she was with him she always enjoyed herself. Look at tonight. When she heard his voice on the phone she had felt so much happier; he had entirely changed her mood simply by showing up out of the blue. He was such fun, so easy-going, so light-hearted.

But is it love? she thought, and couldn't make up her mind. She wasn't sure what love really was—would she know it if she felt it?

She suddenly remembered the odd shiver that had run down her back at the sound of Max's name. At the mere memory, she shivered again, turning pale, then flushing.

What was it she felt for Max? She had only seen him for one day, years ago, and yet when she heard his name she felt weak inside, as though she was falling apart.

Oh, don't be so stupid! she told herself. It was just a teenage crush, over years ago. It wasn't love. How could it have been? Love doesn't happen that fast! Stop thinking about the man. Think about Christos.

What were he and his father doing in London, for instance?

Something secretive, something important, that he couldn't talk about, but in which her father was clearly involved. Whatever it was, it made Christos excited, yet jumpy.

She had the feeling he'd been aching to talk to her about whatever was churning him up, but that he dared not risk it. Christos was very much in awe of his father, and she didn't blame him for that. Constantine Agathios was a very scary man. Christos might say that he cared about her and wanted her to be happy, but Olivia found that hard to credit. Constantine Agathios wasn't fond of her, didn't care about her; if she annoyed him she had the strong feeling he could turn very nasty indeed. There was black temper in that face. No wonder Christos was afraid of annoying him.

Next morning she had hardly walked into the office before the phone began ringing.

'Hello? Public Relations—this is Olivia speaking,' she said, half expecting it to be Christos again.

It was a breezy, assured voice, but not that of Christos. The accent was very much a London one, East End cockney. 'Hello, this is Rodney Fielding, *Daily Globe* newsroom. We've been trying to locate Mr Faulton, to talk to him about this ship going down off the coast of Turkey.'

'One of ours? We don't have any ships in that part of the world, I'm sure we don't,' Olivia said, startled.

'Not one of Faulton's own ships,' agreed the reporter. 'I'm talking about the Agathios Kera line—one of their ferries ran into fog between Greece and Turkey and collided with an oil tanker yesterday morning. Hadn't you heard about it?'

'No,' Olivia said slowly, horrified. 'Did you say the Agathios ship went down?'

'It finally sank this morning; it was crippled, couldn't be salvaged. They got most of the passengers off, but four people died and a dozen or so were injured, mostly burns—there was an explosion on the oil tanker.'

The brisk matter-of-factness of the voice appalled her. 'How terrible,' she said, paling. Only last night she and Christos had talked about oil spillage and an environmental disaster. It was almost as if they had conjured this up out of nowhere; she felt horribly guilty.

Oh, of course it was crazy to think like that! It wasn't her fault, and, thank God, she didn't have to fend off accusing questions, think up bland answers, explanations, apologies, because it was nothing to do with their company, yet she still had a superstitious feeling that somehow she and Christos had made this happen.

'Mr Faulton hasn't mention it to you?' asked the reporter.

'No, but why should he? It really has nothing to do with this company——' she began and the reporter interrupted.

'But he is on the board of Agathios Kera, isn't he?'

Olivia drew a sharp breath. She had forgotten that. 'Oh...yes,' she said slowly. 'But he's in London at the moment, not in Greece, which is the headquarters of the Agathios Kera line.'

'They have an office in London though, don't they? And I'm told they're having a board meeting this morning, to discuss the disaster.'

'Oh, are they?' Olivia was surprised into indiscretion. 'That's news to me. Look, I really can't help you, I'm afraid. I don't even know as much as you do, and I'm new here. I only started work yesterday.' She frowned, then said sharply, 'And anyway, why are you ringing here? Why not ring Agathios Kera's London offices?'

'I tried,' said the reporter cynically. 'It was busy.'

'Then try again!'

'I've been trying for the past hour. The line's engaged all the time. I think they've taken the phone off the hook. Not surprising really—they've had a bad month so far, what with the death of old Kera, and Max Agathios's financial problems...'

'What financial problems?' Olivia felt ice trickling down her spine. She was remembering that conversation she had overhead last week, the odd uneasiness she had felt as she listened.

'You really don't know much about the business, do you?' the reporter said pityingly. 'Look, Agathios borrowed heavily to finance his expansion into the cruise business. Cruise ships are expensive. He's had to invest a lot of money, and because of the recession people haven't been taking cruises.' He paused, laughed and added, 'Agathios has run into bad weather, in fact. What do you bet that that's our headline?'

'A bit obvious, isn't it?' Olivia muttered. She didn't share his sense of humour, but then she was personally involved in all this, and the reporter wasn't. To him this was just a story—he didn't give a damn about the consequences for everyone involved.

'Headlines have to be obvious,' he snapped. 'Anyway, Agathios's partner died at exactly the wrong moment.'

'Is there ever a right moment to die?' Olivia asked bitterly. 'I don't suppose the poor man wanted to die now.'

'Don't suppose he did,' the reporter said cheerfully. 'But he has made life very difficult for Max Agathios. Old Kera has always backed him financially, they've been a successful pair, and Max is going to miss him.'

Olivia was thinking, her face puzzled. 'But what about Mr Kera's daughter? Wasn't she an only child? Won't she inherit everything?'

'Oh, sure, but Opie won't want to put any more money into Agathios Kera.'

Olivia stiffened. 'Opie?' She recognised the name her father had said on the phone the other day. 'Who on earth is Opie?' Was it Daphne Kera's nickname, or something?

'That's the daughter's married name,' the reporter said, and Olivia almost dropped the phone. She sat staring at nothing while the man's voice chattered on in her ear. 'Daphne Kera married an Australian wool exporter. Simon Opie's not interested in shipping, and all his business interests are in Australia, so the rumour is that Daphne Opie will want to sell her share in Agathios Kera—the only question is, who would want to buy?' The reporter's voice had become brisk. 'Got to go. Look, darling, when Faulton gets back, could you give me a buzz, give me a shot at him before anyone else gets the chance? You owe me for all the information I've fed you. And take my advice—if you're going to hold down this new job of yours, you had better bone up on the shipping business fast!'

Olivia put the phone down as he hung up. Her mind was in chaos. What was going on? Her father had lied to her—by omission, at least, if not directly. He had said that Max was definitely going to marry Daphne. But Max hadn't. Daphne had married someone else, an Australian called Simon Opie. Why hadn't Gerald told her that? He must have known.

The phone rang again a few minutes later, and this time she was prepared to find herself talking to another reporter. She rapidly got rid of him, refusing to discuss the subject of Agathios Kera or the ship that had gone down off Turkey, but for the rest of the morning she was dealing with phone calls from various newspapers, all pursuing the same story.

She was relieved to escape to lunch, rather late, leaving the answerphone to take calls, and she didn't hurry back. After a leisurely lunch at a salad bar, she walked back in rather watery sunshine. It suddenly occurred to her that her father might well call in on her, as he was in London, to see how she was coping with her new job. She looked at her watch. Half-past two. The board meeting at Max's offices must surely be over by now? She began to walk faster.

There was no sign of her father though, and when she rang his secretary, Mrs Grange, she was told that Gerald Faulton hadn't yet returned.

'I'm snowed under with messages from newspapers, Mrs Grange,' Olivia said. 'I'm just refusing to comment, but when my father comes in would you ask him to let me know what he wants me to say to the Press about this Agathios Kera business?'

'Well, I'll leave him a message, Miss Faulton, but...well, I have a problem, you see. My little boy's school just rang—they think he has mumps. He's running a high temperature and his jaw has swollen right up. Normally my mother would deal with an emergency like this, but she's away. I'll have to go myself. I'm afraid your father's going to be very irritated.'

'No, of course he won't be, of course you must go,' Olivia said at once.

'Oh, thank you,' Mrs Grange said gratefully. 'I'll get one of the other girls to sit in here and man the phones.'

'I'll do that,' Olivia said at once. 'Switchboard can re-route any calls for me to my father's office. I don't have anything much to do here anyway.'

'Oh, would you? You wouldn't mind?' Mrs Grange's voice was startled. 'But what would your father say about you doing my job?'

'He won't mind, he likes me to take more interest in his business,' Olivia blithely said, yet thought: if he really does, why does he lie to me and keep so much from me? He never tells me anything, and if he does it isn't always the truth.

She collected her things, informed the switchboard that she would be in her father's office for the rest of the afternoon, and walked along the corridor to the large suite of offices Gerald Faulton occupied.

Mrs Grange was just leaving. She had been Gerald's secretary for only a few months, and seemed flustered, still nervous of his reaction to finding out that Olivia had taken over her job for the afternoon. A smartly dressed woman in her late thirties, with smooth dark hair and blue eyes, she was divorced from her husband but devoted to her only child, the boy, Andrew, who had just come down with mumps. Olivia suspected she would not be working there very long. Gerald expected his secretaries to be one-track-minded, to devote themselves to him and his business, not to husbands or children.

'If you could just write down any messages on this pad... and if you have to leave before five-thirty—even if you just pop out to the cloakroom—could you let the switchboard know?' Mrs Grange stammered out, watching Olivia uneasily.

Olivia nodded. 'Don't worry. Off you go, I'll cope here.'

When she was alone she walked out of Mrs Grange's little office into her father's much more spacious room. Olivia wandered around, stroking the panelled walls, pulling out a book here and there from the rows of tomes on shipping and the law in the polished oak bookcase, touching objects on her father's wide, leather-topped desk. She sat in his revolving leather chair, swung round in it, played with his intercom and tried the locked drawers in the desk.

She felt much as she had when she was a child and visited him here. Everything in this room was perfect, austere, placed precisely and always in its place. The room had its personal and particular smell: a mingling of leather and polish and the eau-de-Cologne her father used.

Olivia was almost in a trance, her hands on her father's desk, her head back against the deep leather upholstered chair, staring around her.

Suddenly a voice outside the door said sharply, 'You can't go in there! He isn't there, I tell you!'

Olivia jumped, looking at the door as it opened with a crash and someone came through it so abruptly that it was almost as if they had thrown themselves into the room.

Her golden eyes wide, she stared at Max Agathios.

He had stopped dead and was staring back at her.

The air between them seemed to her to shimmer, like the air in a desert, making Max's image come and go as if he were a mirage, and Olivia almost believed he was, almost thought she was fantasising. He wasn't really there, she had conjured him up because she had been thinking about him so much.

Behind him one of the office girls was babbling, 'I'm sorry, Miss Faulton, I told him Mr Faulton wasn't here, but he wouldn't listen, he forced his way in here. Shall I call the police?'

'No...it's OK...' Olivia managed huskily. 'There's nothing to worry about. I...I'll deal with it.'

The girl seemed uncertain. 'Well, I'll stay out here, in Mrs Grange's office, if you like, in case you need me——'

'Shut the door and get out!' Max snarled, and turned his black head to look at the girl in a way that sent her scurrying.

The door closed on her and Max looked back at Olivia. She had not taken her eyes off him since he erupted into the room. How many years? she was thinking. How many years since she had last seen him, on Corfu, in her father's villa? Not that many. She had been seventeen. Now she was twenty-two. Five years.

She had changed, she knew that; her father had called her a schoolgirl that summer on Corfu, and he had been quite right, she had to admit that now, however reluctantly. That was what she had been, an unawakened, wide-eyed schoolgirl completely out of her depth with a man like Max Agathios. Looking back, she was amazed he hadn't seen it, realised how young and inexperienced she was—surely he must have had some inkling?

Of course, she had been excited by him, trying to act very grown-up under the influence of her first strong sexual attraction, and in that lazy, casual beach atmosphere her true age might not have shown up, especially as neither she nor Max had been wearing very much. Clothes were often a good clue to age and background.

Max's clothes now were a million miles away from the old jeans and T-shirt he had been wearing that day in Corfu. Today his clothes were expensive, exclusive: he wore a smoothly tailored city suit in dark grey pinstripe, and with it a stiff white shirt and maroon tie. He looked formal, as remote as her father, and he had hardened, looked leaner, tougher, as if he had shed some weight, and with it the charm and warmth he had had five years ago, and which she had found irresistible.

She didn't think she liked this icy, hostile stranger.

Quietly, she asked him, 'Why do you want to see my father, Mr Agathios?'

'Why?' he repeated in a harsh, charged voice. Rage blazed out of him, the heat of it hitting her across the room. His black eyes glittered. 'I'm going to kill him!'

CHAPTER FOUR

OLIVIA sucked in air in a startled, incredulous, horrified reaction. Her golden eyes searched his face, looking for a trace of humour, for some evidence that the threat had been a joke, but his features were implacable, tight with anger and that deeply embedded hostility she had seen from the minute he forced his way into this office.

She swallowed, her face white, her eyes all pupil suddenly, a glassy, disturbed blackness eating up the golden glow of the iris.

'What are you talking about?' The whisper of her voice was only just audible in the room.

'You don't know?' The cold sneer in his voice hurt her, told her he despised her, hated her too.

'I wouldn't ask if I did!'

'You're sitting behind your father's desk, you're obviously running this office while he's not here—yet you don't have a clue what I'm talking about? Do you really expect me to believe that?' Max took a long stride and was suddenly on the other side of the desk, only inches away from her. He put both hands on the desk and bent towards her; Olivia flinched back in her chair. From the other side of the room he had been disturbing—this close he was a physical threat she found alarming. 'Don't forget, I remember you making a fool of me the first time we met! You're your father's daughter all right. Well, I don't fall for the same trick twice.'

'I didn't lie to you!' She had not got the chance to tell him that five years ago; she had been waiting ever since to put the record straight. 'I didn't realise you didn't know how old I was! It never occurred to me that you didn't know. You never asked and I didn't think of telling you.'

'I never asked because you looked older and...' He broke off, his face dark with smouldering rage. 'Oh, hell, never mind! I didn't come here to talk about old times. I'm not going to let you distract me from catching up with your father.'

His voice lashed her. To hide her fear, she began to talk far too fast, gabbling out the words. 'I wasn't trying to... I don't work here, I'm just taking over from my father's secretary for the day. Her little boy is ill, she had to go home, and I've just started to work here, in the public relations office...'

She broke off, seeing Max's eyes flash like black lightning.

'Public relations? Which means you deal with the Press.'

'Yes,' she whispered, biting her lip.

'And I've no doubt you've had plenty of calls from them today!' he bit out, and she couldn't deny it.

'Quite a few reporters have rung, yes, wanting to talk to my father, wanting quotes about the board meeting you held this morning, but I was no help to them—I didn't know as much as they did! They told me more than I could tell them!'

Max's mouth writhed bitterly. 'Did they tell you that my brother and your father covet my company, that the two of them conspired to buy up my late partner's shares so that they could get control, manipulate the board and get me kicked off it?'

Olivia felt sick. So that was what her father had been up to with Constantine Agathios?

'Kicked out of my own company!' Max ground out between his teeth. 'The company I built up from nothing, just a few battered old ships that should really have gone to the breaker's yard. Constantine inherited the lion's share of my father's fleet, and yet he resented the fact that my father left me anything at all. He hoped I'd go bankrupt, and I'm well aware that he secretly worked to steal my contracts, competed with me wherever he could, undercut me, lied about me. But I fought back; I worked like a slave to build up new routes, get new contracts, and I managed to find someone who believed in me and was prepared to back me.'

'Leon Kera,' she thought aloud, as he paused, and he gave her a cynical, icy look.

'Oh, you admit you know that much about my operation!'

She hated the contempt in his voice, and her skin tightened. 'I didn't say I knew nothing about you and your company. I said I knew nothing about my father's...plans...the board meeting...'

Her father had made sure she knew nothing, she realised. He had consistently lied to her, shut her out, ever since she had met Max in Corfu five years ago. Hadn't Gerald trusted her not to warn Max? She bit her lip. Well, if she had known, and had seen Max, wouldn't she have had a problem not warning him? How could her father do this? And Max's own brother, too! Cheating him, secretly trying to destroy him, to take his company away from him. Olivia was appalled.

'Leon Kera was the best friend I ever had,' Max said. 'I was lucky to know him; he was a great man. He invested in my company, bought a big block of shares when I went public, and he advised me. It was Leon's idea that we should go into the cruise business, but we weren't lucky with our timing.' He sighed, his mouth grim. 'Costs and interest rates went up steeply and because of the recession passengers cut back on holidays, especially expensive ones like cruises. We've had our problems, but I have no doubt that in another five years we'd have been as solid as a rock.' He stopped, his black brows meeting, his face tense and dark. After a brief pause he went on, 'But Leon died and the vultures moved in on me.'

'But how can they kick you out of your own company?'

He gave her an angry, impatient look. 'Still pretending you don't know a thing about it? I don't buy this innocence of yours. You're your father's daughter, and his only heir. Knowing him, he's been grooming you to take over from him one day. He won't have kept you in ignorance of what he's plotting with my brother!'

'My father never tells me anything.' There was bitterness in Olivia's eyes, in her voice, and Max watched her closely, frowning as though trying to decide whether or not to believe what he was seeing. 'My father doesn't even let his right hand know what his left hand is doing,' she told him, remembering the way her father and Constantine Agathios had thrown her and Christos together.

This summer when she flew in to Nice, she had felt adult, grown up at last, finished with her studies, about to enter the real world, become fully independent. She had thought she was making her own decisions, thought she was a free agent, and all the time she had been as powerless, as impotent, as governed, as a child.

I was their puppet—they pulled my strings, I danced and I didn't even know what was happening to me, she thought, humiliated and angry.

And what about Christos? Was he a puppet too, as hoodwinked as she had been, as manipulated? Or had Christos known what the two older men were up to? Had they ordered him to propose to her? Had he wanted to? Did he care anything about her? What did she really know about Christos?

Max was watching her fixedly, frowning.

'You expect me to believe that?'

Suddenly angry, Olivia met his eyes, her chin up, glaring. 'I don't care what you believe! It doesn't matter whether you believe me or not, but I tell you my father never takes me into his confidence, especially where business is concerned. Just tell me this ... how can my father and your brother take your company away from you?'

Max bared his teeth angrily and ran a hand through his thick, black hair, ruffling it into confusion.

'OK!' he growled. 'OK, I'll play your little game, pretend you don't know. I suppose you're deliberately trying to slow me down, waste time, in the hope that one of those girls out there has called the police—but if that's your game plan, don't think it will save your father, because even if the police arrived they couldn't lock me up, only warn me not to breach the peace, because I haven't done anything. Yet. And sooner or later I would get to your father, even if he hides behind electronic devices and a whole mob of security people. One day I'll get him.'

Olivia believed him. There was such smouldering hatred in his jet eyes. Her hands began to shake and Max looked down at them. She snatched them out of sight, into her lap, trying to control the tremors running through her. She must try to stop him realising just how much he frightened her.

In a flat, clipped voice Max said, 'Leon Kera and I together owned sixty-five per cent of the company, and the rest was held by a lot of smaller shareholders. While Leon was alive I was safe, but the minute he died, my brother and your father got together to buy his shares from his daughter. I'd have bought them myself, if I had had the money, but every penny I have is tied up in the company, and no bank would lend me any more.'

The phone on the desk began to ring and Max broke off. Olivia automatically reached out, but Max got there first. He lifted the receiver, listened, then said tersely, 'Miss Faulton isn't taking any calls, and don't put any more through.'

He slammed the receiver down, the crash making Olivia jump. Max began prowling to and fro like a caged lion. 'Where was I? Oh, yes, I had no idea what was afoot until just before the board meeting. Of course, I knew Constantine coveted my company, but I couldn't believe Daphne would sell to him—she knew her father wouldn't have wanted her to do that.'

His face had an angry cynicism. He stopped in front of the window, staring out, his hands in his trouser pockets, his head back, his face darkly frowning. 'I should have guessed, I should have remembered...a woman scorned is a bad enemy.' He broke off, threw Olivia a swift, hard look and said grimly, 'Emotion is a dangerous ingredient if it gets mixed up in business affairs.'

'I'd heard that you and your partner's daughter were once... There were rumours you were going to marry her. But you didn't?' Olivia didn't like to ask directly what had happened between them, why Daphne Kera had married someone else, and was now deliberately setting out to ruin Max.

He ignored the tentative question, staring out of the window again, his back to her. His voice flat, he went on, 'At the board meeting this morning your father put down a motion calling me irresponsible and incompetent and demanding my resignation as managing director. I suddenly found myself without any friends around that table. They voted for my brother to take over running the company.'

Olivia watched the line of his back under that formal, elegant suit. He looked much better naked, she thought, remembering the first time she saw him, on the beach, that day in Corfu—and felt heat leap inside her. She mustn't think about that day. She must concentrate on what he had just said. Max was right. Emotion was a dangerous ingredient in business affairs.

Huskily, she asked, 'But...can they really do that? Take your company away from you? Couldn't you fight them? Can't your lawyers do something to stop them?'

He turned slowly, his brows lifted, giving her a long, incredulous look. 'I am almost tempted to believe you mean it—you really don't know anything!'

'I told you I didn't! Only what I've read or been told by the Press!'

He searched her face, then his mouth indented. 'I must be crazy, believing you! You're your father's daughter, one day you'll be running all this——' he gestured around the room '—and now you'll have my company too!'

'I don't want your company!'

He laughed bitterly. 'Well, you've got it. Or your father has, which will come to the same thing one day.'

'But...what about your shares in the company?'

He shrugged. 'Oh, they can't take my shares away. I still own more than thirty per cent, and if I can get a public shareholders' meeting I might still make them take me back on the board, but I can't make them give me back my job as managing director. Together, they own the majority of shares. That's why they're directors—I invited them all on to the board, that's the irony of it. Now they're kicking me out, and there is nothing I can do to stop it, nothing any lawyer can do either. I've lost my company and my brother has finally got what he has been coveting ever since our father died. Constantine has won.'

'For the moment,' Olivia softly said, wishing he wouldn't stand so close. She was more and more aware of him; the lean, powerful body was hard to ignore. Every time he moved, even breathed, her pulses reacted, shocking her because she hadn't expected him to have that effect on her, not now, not any more. Five years ago she had been easy to impress. She hadn't had a boyfriend, was a wide-eyed innocent. Max had had a walkover with her. She'd grown up since then. She shouldn't be getting these waves of intense awareness.

Max leaned even closer, staring down into her golden eyes. 'Yes,' he slowly said. 'For the moment.'

'I'm sure you'll fight back.' He wasn't the type to give up a fight and just walk away. Max was a fighter; every tough bone in his body told you that, every pugnacious line in his face.

He half-smiled. 'I'm sure too, but if you're hoping to hear about any plans I might have, you can forget it. I'm not that stupid. I know that anything I say to you will go straight back to your father and my brother.'

Stung, she burst out, 'No! I won't even tell them I've seen you!'

There was a long silence while their eyes were locked. 'Won't you, Olivia?' he drawled. 'If I believed you, I might wonder why.'

She looked down, her lashes cloaking her eyes. 'They'd keep asking me endless questions. I...I don't want to be cross-examined; I don't want to get involved in any of this! I hate it, plots and back-stairs politics and——'

Max abruptly said, 'Is it true that you're going to marry my nephew?'

She had wondered if he knew. Huskily, she admitted, 'Yes, we got engaged last week.'

'Are you in love with him?' She hated the contemptuous twist of his mouth as he said that, and a dark flush crept up her face.

'I'm not discussing my personal life!'

'If you were in love with him, why would you mind admitting it?'

She tensed, realising how true that was, but defiantly threw back, 'If I wasn't, why would I get engaged to him?'

'Any number of reasons,' Max drily said. 'You might be ambitious, and there's no doubt Christos is a good catch—he's going to be very rich, one day. You could simply get married and think Christos would make a suitable husband, or you might have been badgered into it by your father——'

'No! He didn't!' Olivia might be angry with her father for the way he'd manipulated her and her life, but she couldn't discuss it with Max. That would be too disloyal, not to mention humiliating. 'My father would never badger me into anything!'

Max smiled cynically. 'No, I suppose not. He has other techniques for dealing with you, doesn't he? He freezes you into submission. If you disobey him he puts you in deep freeze until you're ready to do whatever he wants.'

He was far too shrewd; he saw too much, heard what you did not say; she almost began to think he could read minds, and Olivia found him even more worrying than her father, because she suddenly knew that Max Agathios could hurt her far more than her father ever had. 'I think you'd better go,' she broke out shakily. 'My father won't be back for hours; there's no point in your waiting.'

He considered her, his face cool and blank, then nodded. 'You mean it scares you even to talk about it? Isn't it time you found the courage to run your own life, Olivia? Make your own decisions, choose your own friends and lovers?'

She kept her eyes averted, didn't risk answering, but the stiff mask of her face was probably answer enough because Max laughed shortly.

'Well, give your father a message from me—tell him he may think he has got away with it, but I haven't given up; I'll get him if it's the last thing I do!'

He turned away and began to walk to the door. Olivia got up, intending to follow him and ask one of the junior secretaries to take over from her in her father's office, because she needed some time alone, she had to think. But just as his hand reached for the door-handle Max suddenly swung round again, making her nerves jump.

'That girl who tried to stop me coming in here will tell him I came,' he said tersely. 'So you'd better mention it first, or he'll wonder why you didn't say anything.'

She frowned, realised he was right, nodded without speaking, and that nod made them conspirators.

Max watched her, his eyes brilliant, searching hers as if looking for something in their golden depths. She tried to glance away and couldn't; she was trapped in the beam

of his stare like a rabbit in headlights, her heart beating
far too fast.

Max strode back towards her, took hold of her face
with one hand, tilted her head back, while his other hand
went round her waist, pulling her towards him.

It all happened too fast. She had no time to think, let
alone stop him. His head came down and his mouth hit
hers.

The kiss was fatal, a bullet to the heart. She felt her
whole body jerk in shock, in a mixture of agony and
intense pleasure. Her eyes stayed wide open, fixed, desperate, her skin was ice-cold, her mouth was burning.
She was dying, shaking, her hands reaching out to hold
on to him to stop herself falling down. She clutched his
shirt and swayed, the only part of her that was still alive
her mouth, kissing him back.

As suddenly as he had begun to kiss her he stopped,
lifting his head, moving away.

She stood there, still wide-eyed, still white, still helpless in anguish.

Max stared at her, breathing fiercely, his skin dark
red.

'Now at least you'll know what you missed,' he said
between tight teeth. 'They coveted my company—even
if you marry my nephew, you'll always remember I
coveted you.'

Then he was gone, moving so fast she blinked as if at
a lightning flash. The door slammed. Olivia felt her way
around the desk like a blind man, sank back into the
chair. Her ears were ringing. Her blood was roaring
through her veins. She thought she was going to faint.
She put her head down on the desk.

It seemed only a second later that the door crashed
open again. She thought at first that Max had come back,

and sat up in a hurry, flushed, distraught, her blonde hair tangled, her eyes wide.

'Olivia! My God, you look… What did he do to you?'

It was Christos, darkly flushed, anger in his eyes as he almost ran across the room.

Behind him she saw Constantine Agathios, glowering, heavy, his bull's head lowered as if he were going to charge, and her father, narrow-eyed, hard-faced, watching her as if he suspected, could guess, at what had happened, her emotional turmoil.

Christos came round the desk and bent down to look into her face. 'It's OK, Olivia, don't look like that… He's gone, and he'll never come anywhere near you again.'

She burst into tears and Christos put his arms around her, pulled her against him, held her like a child, stroking her hair, murmuring softly.

'Don't, darling, don't cry like that, you're safe now…'

She wasn't safe; she would never be safe again. That kiss had changed everything, her whole world was upside down and she couldn't tell Christos—how could she? What could she say? That she had realised she couldn't marry him because she could never love him? The fondness she felt for Christos would never turn into love—she had let herself think it might, had deceived herself, but she couldn't any more because that kiss had forced her to face the truth.

The intensity of her reaction had been a blinding shock, ripping away all her pretences, illusions, defences.

She clung to Christos, her face buried in his shirt, wondering desperately how she was going to get out of her engagement. Would it hurt his feelings when she told him? Did he really care?

'Pull yourself together, Olivia!' her father said in his cold, incisive voice. 'Let go of her, Christos! Here, take this, Olivia, wipe your face and blow your noise, snap out of it!'

He thrust a box of paper tissues into her hand, gestured to Christos to move away, then leaned on the edge of the desk, watching her as she shakily obeyed him, dried her damp face, wiped her eyes, blew her nose, dropped the used tissues into the wastepaper basket under the desk.

'Got a comb?' Gerald Faulton asked curtly. 'Use it, tidy yourself up, then you can tell us what Max was doing here, what he wanted, what he said.'

Olivia kept her eyes down, fumbled in her bag, found a compact, a comb, make-up, and did a repair job on her face. When her hair was smooth again, her lipstick renewed, her nose powdered, she sat up and felt able to meet her father's inimical eyes.

He had never loved her, she thought, staring back at him; all her life she had known that. Cold, bleak, rejecting, he had made it impossible for her to love him. It would be easier to bear if she knew why. What had she done to make her own father dislike her? Why, if he disliked her, did he keep in touch, make her spend those holidays with him every year? Duty, as her mother said?

'Now,' Gerald Faulton said, 'what happened?'

'You obviously know—he came here, he was looking for you, he was angry, very angry...' She tried to make her voice level and calm but it shook. 'He said...that he was going to kill you.' Max wanted him to know that. He wanted her to tell her father he had made that threat, or she wouldn't have told Gerald.

'Did he hurt you?' Christos asked, still looking anxious.

She glanced at him, her golden eyes sad, because she was fond of him, she liked him, Christos was a darling, but he was never going to be able to set her on fire. The way Max had, she thought, her pulses haywire. Oh, God, the way he had. That terrible power he had over her—the power of life and death. That kiss had unlocked the doors of heaven and hell. She had died under the touch of his mouth—and yet, too, she had been dead for years, and that kiss had brought her back to life.

'Hurt me?' she repeated, with wild irony. 'Oh, no, he didn't hurt me.' He just destroyed me, she thought.

'Then what was all the drama about?' bit out her father.

'Obviously, he frightened the life out of her,' protested Christos. 'Threatening to kill you ... shouting the place down, according to that girl out there, who heard his voice going on and on for ages, bullying Olivia. No wonder she was upset.'

Constantine Agathios interrupted, his heavy-lidded eyes intent on her. 'Did he tell you what he planned to do now?'

'I told you what he said ... he threatened to kill my father.'

Gerald impatiently said, 'Yes, yes, that's just a lot of hot air. He's far too clever to do anything of the sort and get locked up for life. Did he say anything else? Did you pick up any idea what he means to do now?'

She shook her head. 'No idea at all. I did ask him what he was going to do, and he said he wasn't going to tell me because I would only tell you.'

The two older men glanced at each other. Constantine brooded, his head down, his mouth a heavy line.

'What can he do?' asked Christos, shrugging. 'You have a majority on the board, you own more voting shares than he does... He's finished now, what can he do?'

'I wish I knew,' his father grunted. 'Max is as slippery as an eel. I still feel uneasy. I just wish I knew what he was up to!'

'Oh, come on,' said her father impatiently, 'he can't hurt us! We outgun him. While the two of us hold more shares, he's helpless.'

'Let's hope you're right,' Constantine said, but he did not look very reassured.

Olivia listened, her face blank but her mind very busy. Max might have lost control of his company, they might have out-manoeuvred him for the moment, but it was crystal-clear that he still worried his brother, who was uneasy, twitchy, afraid that Max still had an ace up his sleeve and could still beat them, somehow, some way. Logically, they had won, as her father had just said, but Constantine's own gut instincts, and his knowledge of his younger half-brother, warned him not to be too complacent, and Olivia was sure he was right to worry.

'You're superstitious about him!' Gerald Faulton muttered, frowning. 'You seem to think he has magical powers—but he doesn't, man! He isn't the devil incarnate. It's all in your own head! I tell you, he can't do anything about it. For one thing, he hasn't any money, unless he sells his own shares in the company.'

'He'd never do that!' Constantine grimaced. 'That would be admitting he had no hope of getting it back.'

'Well, there you are then!'

Christos had been listening to them, his face thoughtful. Suddenly he said, 'He could sell Hymnos!'

'What?' Gerald Faulton stared at Christos. 'Sell what?'

'I'd forgotten all about it,' Constantine said slowly, staring at his son. 'But you're right—he could raise money by selling Hymnos. Clever of you to think of it, Christos!'

'What are you both talking about?' Gerald asked, pale and frowning.

Constantine turned towards him. 'Along with his ships, my brother inherited an island from my father— it isn't very big, and it isn't inhabited, although Max has built himself a house on it, I gather, but these days, with Greek tourism growing by leaps and bounds, a small island in the Aegean could be very valuable. I've no doubt he could find a buyer, and he might raise a considerable sum by selling it.'

Gerald said shortly, 'Even so, there's nothing he can do. Oh, he could buy up a few of the smaller shareholders, but we'll still be in control because we have the majority shareholding.' He gave Constantine a cool, rueful look. 'Stop getting so worked up about him! We're as safe as houses.'

Constantine let out a long sigh. 'Yes, you're right, of course you are.'

Christos dreamily said, 'I've always envied him, owning Hymnos. I'd love an island of my own, wouldn't you, Olivia?'

His father gave him an indulgent smile. 'Well, if Max does put it on the market, I may buy it for you—if the price is right!'

A few weeks later Gerald walked into Olivia's office and threw down on her desk a folded copy of *The Times*.

'He did it! Look at that—I've ringed it. It seems you and Christos may be going to get a Greek island for a wedding present!'

Dazedly she picked up the newspaper and looked at the red-ringed property advertisement.

'FOR SALE: a floating Garden of Eden', the estate agency announced. 'The small island of Hymnos in the Aegean sea, with only one moderately sized house, with all modern conveniences, electricity generator supplying power to house, bathrooms, fully equipped kitchen, up-to-date radio equipment for emergencies, helicopter pad, boathouse, swimming-pool and well maintained paddocks—the perfect hideaway for the man who has everything except perfect privacy. Unmatched views, within two hours' sailing distance of nearest airport. To be sold at auction, all details supplied by agent.'

She slowly looked up. 'I don't imagine Christos's father really meant what he said. I can't see him buying some remote Greek island that is obviously going to cost a fortune, judging by all the expensive toys on it—helicopter pad, radio equipment, boathouse—heaven knows what price it will fetch at auction.'

Gerald's cold mouth twisted. 'If Max Agathios inherited it from their father, Constantine will want it. Surely you've realised how much Constantine hates Max? The two of them take sibling rivalry to a new height.'

Christos rang her at her flat that evening. 'My father's going to that auction!' he told her excitedly, and she drew a sharp breath.

'He was serious about buying it?'

'You bet he was! He's always resented the fact that Grandpapa left Hymnos to Max, not him, and nothing is going to stop him getting it at last. So he isn't going to leave it to intermediaries, he's going there himself, to make sure nothing goes wrong and someone outbids him...and he suggests we go with him. The auction is to be held on the island itself—apparently the auctioneers plan to take people over by helicopter. There won't be a large group of bidders involved, at the starting price Max has set, but Dad plans to sail over there on his yacht, the *Agathios Athena*, so that we can see Hymnos for ourselves before the auction.'

Pale, reluctant, Olivia murmured, 'But...I've only just started working here. I don't think my father would let me have the time off!'

'He's coming too,' said Christos. 'Dad talked to him a few minutes ago. We'll all fly over to Greece; *Agathios Athena* is tied up at Piraeus, we'll sail the day we arrive, spend one day at Hymnos, then sail back to Piraeus and fly to London again. It should only take three days—a long weekend, that's all. And your father has already said you could come, don't worry, so that's OK. It will be fun.'

Olivia rang off a few minutes later and looked at her own white face in the mirror.

She did not want to go to Hymnos, to watch Max's private paradise being sold to his brother. What if Max was there? She closed her eyes, biting her lip.

She wished she had the courage to tell Christos she didn't love him and she was sure he was not in love with her either, break off her engagement, face up to her father's rage.

But she didn't dare. Christos might not be heartbroken, but he was fond of her, he might be upset, and he would certainly be frightened of his father's reaction. So was she. Constantine terrified her. Almost as much as her father. When Gerald found out, he would be icy, implacable. He wanted her to marry Christos to cement his alliance with Constantine; if she didn't, he would never forgive her.

Oh, if only she weren't such a coward!

CHAPTER FIVE

OLIVIA hadn't been back to the Greek islands since that last holiday with her father on Corfu. As the plane began to descend to land at Athens airport, that October afternoon, she looked out of the window and saw the blue Aegean far below her, the autumnal colouring of the mountainous landscape behind Athens, and felt a sudden dart of *déjà vu*. Just over five years ago she had flown into Corfu, looked down on blue seas and green and brown mountains, felt a surge of excitement and anticipation. Greece had a light all its own; nowhere else had this immense clarity, a radiance like that of heaven. She felt the same surge again, and then just as suddenly sadness welled up inside her. That time she flew into Corfu she hadn't yet met Max, she was just looking forward to some weeks in the sun. Today she felt none of that eager excitement. Instead, she felt sick with guilt, with worry.

In front of her she saw Constantine's lowered, bull-like head, her father beside him reading a newspaper. Christos was sitting beside her. They had flown over here on Constantine's small private plane.

They had come to take another of Max's possessions away from him, something else he loved and they coveted—his private paradise, the advertisement in the newspaper had called it.

It must be agonising for Max to sell it. No wonder he was full of hate, for his brother, for her father. For her too? she wondered, and winced at the thought.

She shouldn't have come. She should have made some excuse, refused to go. It had been in her mind to do just that, but she had met her father's cold, level stare and the words had dried up in her throat.

Why am I such a coward? she silently accused herself, her eyes burning with unshed tears of self-contempt.

It was only as they began to come down through the clouds that they saw the smog hovering over the city; thick, yellow, damp, enveloping the Parthenon, the tree-crowned hills beside it, the Agora and the old houses of the Plaka, swirling around the tops of modern glass and concrete office blocks, making it impossible to see more than a few yards ahead.

'London used to get these fogs, years ago,' Olivia said to Christos, 'until they brought in the clean air laws and stopped people using coal, either in domestic fires or industry. Now smog is a thing of the past, thank heavens.'

Christos shrugged. 'Modern living has so many problems, and it all happened so rapidly in Greece that we're still coping with the shock of the modern. At the moment, they're desperately trying to do something about the number of cars coming into the city—in the last twenty years the number of people living here has grown beyond belief, and they all have cars! Traffic is often jammed solid, especially in the centre. Whatever they try, people find a way round it though. They're determined to use their cars, although they're the first to complain about traffic-jams. By the end of this century I wouldn't be surprised to find private cars being banned from entering the centre of the city at all.'

Olivia nodded soberly. 'In London too. The car is becoming a nightmare, isn't it, if you live in a big city?'

Although it was October, it was still very hot, and as they made their way through the terminal sweat began to trickle down Olivia's back under her white shirt. It had been cold and windy in London, and the abrupt change in the weather was a shock, even though she had expected it to be warmer here, and had brought light clothes to wear on the yacht.

It took ages to drive to Piraeus in the yellowish smog. As she got out of the car on the dockside Olivia was stunned by the sheer size of Constantine Agathios's yacht. Remembering Max's boat, she had expected something much smaller, but this huge white yacht was like a small cruise ship—and had, she discovered as they went aboard, a crew of seven, including a chef and two stewards to serve food and drink and clean the cabins, who all lined up on the deck to welcome them to the *Agathios Athena*.

'Dad uses it to impress people,' Christos murmured, grinning at her. 'Politicians, clients, business partners. He calls it a legitimate business expense!'

It must cost a small fortune just to pay the mooring fees, thought Olivia, following him along a panelled corridor.

'This is your cabin,' Christos said, opening a door, and she looked into a small but well equipped room with a porthole window which was the only indication that they were on a ship. The furniture was elegant, even if kept to a minimum, leaving the middle of the room empty, to give the illusion of space. A narrow bed, with a low cabinet beside it holding a bedside lamp, a wardrobe, a dressing-table which could double as a table, were all set into the golden oak panelling on the walls, for stability when the boat hit bad weather, no doubt. Curtains and bedcovers matched, the material a light

blue sprinkled with tiny flowers in pale pink and green,
the same material also covering the small easy chair
which was the only other piece of furniture in the room.

The impression was light, airy, charming. Christos
stood in the doorway, watching her face, as Olivia looked
around.

'Like it?'

She turned to smile at him. 'It's lovely. Amazing how
so much was got into such a tiny room, and yet it looks
quite spacious.'

'Dad had the best Greek yacht designer. If there is one
thing we Greeks know about, it is ships. We were sailing
the seven seas before the British stopped using coracles!'
Christos was half joking, half serious.

'Chauvinist!' teased Olivia and he laughed, a little
flushed but defiant.

'Well, why not? We all have our national pride, don't
we? You can't say Britain doesn't!'

'True,' she said seriously. 'But we're all Europeans
now. I can't wait for the day when we stop talking about
our national pasts and start looking to our shared future.'

Christos grimaced at her. 'Maybe we should—but
whether or not we ever will is anybody's guess. Old habits
die hard. I think the tribal instinct in all of us is the real
problem. It's in our genetic blueprint; we can't argue
ourselves out of it.'

'Argue yourselves out of what?' a sharp voice asked
from behind him.

They hadn't heard Gerald Faulton walking past.
Christos swung round, startled, and Olivia tensed. Her
father had always had that effect on her, she thought
grimly. When had she ever felt at ease with him?

'Olivia and I were just talking politics,' said Christos
cheerfully. 'I guess you could call it that. She's a strong

European—I'm not so sure it is going to work, politically.'

'Economics is what the common market is all about,' Gerald coldly informed him, his tone, his manner, leaving no room for discussion. 'And it has to work, for all our sakes. Are you coming up on deck to watch us sail?'

'I've done it a hundred times. I'll skip it this time; I have some phone calls to make,' Christos said, looking faintly sulky because Gerald had talked to him in a dictatorial way. He was used to that from his own father; he didn't see why he should put up with it from hers. 'What about you, Olivia?'

'I'd like to,' she admitted. 'I've never done it before.'

Christos grinned at her indulgently. 'OK. Mind you, in this fog, you won't be able to see much. I'll see you in the lounge for cocktails before dinner, in an hour, OK?'

Up on deck, Olivia leaned on the rail beside her father, watching as the port of Piraeus disappeared from view.

The big ships, the masts of shabby fishing boats, the harbour walls, and beyond that the rows of tavernas and little bars whose yellowish lights looked like the eyes of cats in the fog, vanished all at the same time as if eaten up, and suddenly the yacht was alone in rolling banks of soundless, clammy sea mist. Olivia shivered, and her father gave her a sideways frown.

'You should have put a sweater on. This mist isn't very pleasant, is it? Let's go inside. You had better change into something special for dinner—Constantine will expect it.'

She had known that—Christos had warned her to bring at least one dress suitable for a party. She went to her cabin, showered, put on the light green frothy chiffon, and an hour later joined her father in the elegantly furnished lounge where one of the stewards was mixing cocktails in a silver shaker. He turned, smiling, to ask what she would like to drink. Olivia asked for some lime and sparkling mineral water. Her father gave her a bleak look.

'Don't drink much, do you?'

'Not really. An occasional glass of wine, that's all.'

'Your mother didn't either,' grunted Gerald Faulton. 'She was a health fanatic before they invented the term.'

His drink arrived, a dry martini, which came stiff with ice which chinked as he lifted the glass to his mouth.

'Personally, I like a drink,' he muttered, skating a glance over her, taking in the well-brushed blonde hair, the low-cut green chiffon, around her throat the single string of good pearls which he had given her for her eighteenth birthday, in her ears the matching pearl studs he had given for another birthday and on her wrist a pearl and silver bracelet he had given her last year.

She had worn them all tonight, deliberately.

He didn't pay her any compliments, but he did nod approvingly, before taking another swallow of martini.

Olivia wasn't surprised. She would have been surprised if he had said something nice to her.

Her face wry, she sank with a swish of long skirts into one of the deeply upholstered sofas arranged around a low teak coffee-table.

'How long will it take us to reach Hymnos?'

'We should moor off the island tonight,' Gerald said. 'Within an hour or so, at this speed.'

'We are moving fast, aren't we? Yet the whole boat is really steady. Christos says his father had it designed by someone who is the top of the field.'

'No doubt he did,' Gerald said tersely. He did not own a yacht; obviously he didn't approve of Constantine having one, especially such a beautiful and expensive yacht. There was a puritanical streak in him that found it an affront to watch people enjoying themselves, especially if it meant spending large sums of money on their pleasure.

Olivia looked around the lounge, noticing that the table-top had a low rim around it to stop anything placed on it from rolling off, and the furniture had specially shaped feet at all four corners. The feet clicked into place in metal circles set in the woodblock floor.

In heavy seas that would help keep the furniture steady, stop it shifting with the roll of the yacht, yet it could be removed quickly and easily for cleaning purposes.

'Whoever he was, the designer was very ingenious,' she said.

Her father ignored the remark. In his cold, precise voice he said, 'We won't land until tomorrow morning, when everyone else who is interested will fly in by helicopter. There's to be a picnic lunch, which the agency is supplying, and then the auction in the afternoon, in the house itself. Apparently there's only a rough track up to the house from the small cove where we shall have to land, so we'll have to walk up there. I hope it isn't too far. I gather there is a four-wheel-drive vehicle on the island, which Max Agathios uses for driving around the whole place, but it is locked up in a garage and the agent said he didn't have permission to let anyone else use it.'

'Will he be there?'

'The agent? Of course.' Gerald gave her an impatient look.

'No...Max Agathios...' Flushed, Olivia kept her eyes down on her drink, knowing that her father was watching her closely.

She wished she knew what he was thinking, but she had always found that cold mask of his unreadable, except on the occasions when he meant her to realise he was angry with her.

'I've no idea,' Gerald said curtly, and although she didn't look at him she heard the angry undertone. Gerald did not want her to be interested in Max Agathios—there was suspicion and resentment in his voice.

Why did he hate Max? What had Max ever done to him? She couldn't ask, knew he wouldn't answer if she did; her father was intensely secretive about every aspect of his life.

Constantine arrived, heavy and glowering in evening dress, like an overweight penguin. He took the other corner of Gerald's sofa, told the steward to make him a Manhattan, then threw an assessing glance over Olivia, much as her father had done.

Unlike Gerald though, he commented on the way she looked. 'That's a very pretty dress, Olivia—it suits you, you should wear more clothes like that—glamorous, romantic. I like to see you in it.'

He accepted his glass from the steward and lifted it in a silent toast to her, adding, 'Women don't wear romantic clothes any more, I don't know why—all this feminism, I suppose. They want to look like men, which is ridiculous. A woman should look like a woman, not go around in jeans and T-shirts all day.'

Olivia felt irritation burn in her throat, but didn't say what she wanted to say. She knew she looked good in jeans and a T-shirt, and from the way men looked at her they usually thought so too. But she couldn't face an argument with Constantine Agathios, any more than she could with her own father. Coward! she thought. I'm such a coward—and despised herself.

Constantine frowned, glancing around. 'Why isn't Christos here? What's he doing? He knows what time I like dinner to be served.' He reached for the phone on a table beside him. 'In his cabin, I suppose, day-dreaming, instead of getting dressed. I'll give him a ring, tell him to get down here.' He dialled, took a sip of his drink with the phone in one hand, frowned even more as he listened. 'His line's engaged. Who is he ringing, at this hour?'

'He said he had to make a business call,' Olivia hurriedly said.

'Business call! Gossiping with his friends, that's what he means, and at my expense. He went to school in Athens, he still has a lot of friends there. I should have known that the minute he got back to Greece he would be on the phone to them all.'

Constantine swung his heavy head towards the steward discreetly standing at a distance, pretending not to be eavesdropping. 'Here . . . you! Go and find my son and tell him to get along here at once!'

'Yes, sir,' said the steward expressionlessly, moving away, but Olivia jumped up, putting her glass down on the coffee-table, her skirts swishing around her.

'I'll go!' She was dying to get away from the two older men—this was the perfect excuse.

She went out of the sliding glass doors on to the deck and walked towards the door which led to the gangway down to the cabins on the deck below, then halted as she realised that the weather conditions were quite different now.

They had sailed out of the mist. Around them lay blue sea, blue sky, a shimmering horizon with the pale wraith of the moon far out in the distance although it was still light enough to see for miles. There was no sign of land

anywhere. The engines throbbed smoothly in the engine-
room down below. The yacht was moving very fast,
although the stabilisers with which it was fitted dis-
guised its speed. Constantine wanted to reach Hymnos
before nightfall. There were hazards under the waters
around the island, he had said earlier, hidden rocks which
could be very dangerous. The yacht's captain would
prefer the chance to arrive in daylight and moor safely
in the small natural bay.

Olivia leaned on the polished rail, watching the water
churning alongside the hull of the yacht, white foam
tossed like chiffon on the crest of the deep blue waves.
While she gazed down, she saw Max's face form on the
surface of the water, his black eyes staring at her,
accusing her, angry, compelling.

Her heart clenched in pain.

She couldn't bear the idea of seeing him when they
went ashore on Hymnos next day, feeling the lance of
his bitter eyes. Oh, surely he wouldn't want to be there
when they sold his island? Especially if he realised that
his brother was planning to bid for it? Constantine had
informed the auctioneers that he was arriving by sea and
if they knew, Max would know.

She straightened and hurried off to find Christos, but
met him on his way from his cabin.

'They sent me to find you,' she warned, and he
grimaced.

'Dad getting nasty because I was late, was he? I forgot
the time, I was so busy talking to my friends.'

'He said you would be—I told him you were making
business calls!'

Christos grinned, put an arm around her, squeezed
her warmly and kissed her hair. 'You're an angel! Well,
come on—he can only kill me once!'

He was lucky that evening. When they reached the lounge Constantine was on the phone himself, talking in harsh, angry Greek to someone while Gerald silently listened. Olivia couldn't understand a word, but she didn't need to speak the language to understand the tone.

Constantine was furious about something! He slammed the phone down and turned to them with heavy black brows down over his glittering eyes.

'They've put the auction off until the day after tomorrow!'

'Can they do that?' bit out Gerald.

'You heard me trying to force them to change their minds, but it was no use, they had their heels dug in.'

'Why have they done it?' Gerald was narrow-eyed, hard with suspicion.

Constantine eyed him with sardonic irony. 'That was what I wanted to know. Illness, they said—the auction-eer went down with food poisoning today, but should be better within twenty-four hours.'

'Ridiculous. They could get someone else. Max is behind this—I wonder what he's really up to?'

Constantine looked grim. 'I wonder.'

They had dinner a few minutes later. Olivia wasn't hungry. After eating a little clear chicken consommé followed by a seafood salad, she skipped dessert. While the two older men sat over coffee in the lounge, Olivia and Christos went for a walk around the deck in the moonlight, but after a few minutes he looked at his watch with an exclamation.

'I forgot... there's another call I want to make... I won't be five minutes, Olivia, wait here...'

He vanished down the gangway to his cabin and Olivia leaned on the rail. The sea was no longer just an empty blue expanse—ahead of them loomed a dark shape which rapidly became a small island. It had a rocky headland, climbing hills behind it, the silvery grey-green of olive trees fluttering ghostlike in the moonlight, and here and there down the steep cliffs pines swaying gently in the breeze.

With a jab of shock, Olivia wondered, was this Hymnos? She hurried off to her own cabin to find a pair of binoculars she had brought with her, and came back on deck to focus on the island, get a clearer view.

The rocks were a strange colour, a terracotta red streaked with black, barbaric in colour and texture, the grain of the rock geometric, angular, jutting sharply in all directions, with rough grass and broom sprouting in crevices.

The binoculars up to her eyes, she searched the line of the cliffs but could see no sign of habitation. Max's house must be on the other side of the island.

On the rocky headland though, she saw movement. At first she thought it was a tree. Then she realised that it was a man. His arms were lifted, as if he was waving to her. She adjusted the focus of the binoculars, made his image sharper. She couldn't see his face, but she could see the way his thick hair blew backwards in the wind; hair as black as night, curling, rippling like seaweed against the sea-blue light of the moonlit sky. He was wearing black too; like his hair, his shirt blew back in the wind, loose of his black jeans, almost as if it were a cape. His arms were still lifted, the full sleeves of his shirt flapping around them.

Max? she thought, her body shuddering in shock.

Was it Max? Or did she just want it to be him? At this distance she couldn't be sure, but there was something intensely familiar about the black hair, the way he moved. It could be her imagination, though.

Behind him the sky was changing: clouds gathering, just one or two at first, drifting threads of smoky colour, black, grey, smouldering red, more and more of them, until the whole horizon turned dark with approaching storm.

The man on the headland let his arms drop, but stood there for a moment, staring down towards the yacht.

Could he see her? she wondered. He had no binoculars, but from that height he could no doubt see for miles.

Had he been waving to warn her about the coming storm? He must have seen that coming too, long before she did.

Behind her she heard hurrying footsteps and Christos appeared at her side, out of breath, flushed.

'Sorry about that, darling. Were you bored?'

'No, I've been watching the weather, it's changing again,' she said, and Christos threw a look at the sky, frowning.

'You're right—looks as if we might be in for a little rough weather.'

The man on the headland had vanished when Olivia looked back up there a moment later. The island looked empty again.

Within half an hour the storm hit them, buffeting the yacht violently. In spite of its stabilisers, the boat rolled and wallowed in the great black waves. Gerald Faulton looked a ghastly colour as he lurched to his feet and staggered off without a word to his cabin.

'Seasick, poor Gerald!' grinned Constantine, himself perfectly at ease with the mountainous seas. 'Never been seasick in my life, thank God. How about you, Olivia?' He scrutinised her, nodded approval of her colour. 'You look fine, good girl, but you'd better lie down in your cabin all the same. It's easier to cope with rough weather

if you're lying down, and we've no idea when this storm
will blow itself out. We're going to try to battle our way
round into the shelter of Hymnos—inside the little bay
we should be quite safe. Try and get to sleep. By the
morning the weather should be fine again.'

Olivia found the storm exhilarating. Before she went
down to her cabin she stopped to look up at the island.
They were much closer now; she could see the sheer cliffs
towering above them, the sea pounding the rocky beaches
at their base. The yacht was turning, shifting, as the
captain tried to bring it round the point of the island,
into the calmer waters of the bay. Olivia held on tightly
to the rail as the deck swayed and creaked under her
feet.

Her fine green chiffon skirts whisked around her legs
in the wind, then suddenly ballooned upwards, across
her face, blinding her, the delicate gauzy material half
suffocating her as it blew into her mouth. It was like
walking into a spider's web. Olivia shuddered and let go
of the rail to push the skirts down. At that instant the
yacht plunged down into a great cleft between high
waves; the sea washed over the rail and hit Olivia, making
her gasp in shock.

The deck was awash with water. Becoming alarmed,
Olivia turned to hurry down to her cabin, but her feet
slid from under her, and she was flung sideways with
such violence that although she grabbed for the rail as
she fell against it her hands couldn't grip it, her body
went on falling, toppling over.

As she fell overboard she screamed, but the gale caught
her voice and tore it away soundlessly.

Nobody else had been on deck; the attention of the
crew would all be focused in the wheelhouse. Nobody
would know what had happened to her.

Olivia was too shocked to swim at first. She struggled crazily in the water, screaming, but the yacht had already moved on, was too far away for anyone to hear her.

The sea was strangely warm, after a long, hot summer, but the waves were as high as mountains. They rose and fell, crashing down on her relentlessly, dragging her backwards and forwards with them, like human flotsam, her skirts drifting on top of the water like seaweed for a moment, until they slowly filled with water and grew heavy.

A coldness invaded her brain, made her stop panicking, start to think.

When she fell the yacht had been turning into the lee of the island. She must be close to shore; there might be rocks nearby, or a strong tide which might carry her into shore.

She fought to stay calm, let herself float, lifting her head to look towards the island; it towered above her, rocky, inhospitable, yet the only hope she had.

She struck out towards it, fighting the waves which kept hitting her, forcing her backwards. Every time she lifted her head to check on the dark shape of the island she seemed no nearer. For every foot of progress she made, the sea forced her back again. She began to tire; her arms and legs aching, too heavy to lift, she was exhausted, weeping; she couldn't keep going. She couldn't swim another foot.

She was going to drown, here, off Max's island paradise, and nobody would ever know what had happened to her.

CHAPTER SIX

OLIVIA came back to life in agony, lying face down on sand, coughing and choking, her open mouth spewing water, her lungs heaving, her body shuddering violently.

When the convulsions stopped she lay weeping, not knowing where she was or what had happened to her, until strong hands turned her over on to her back.

Wet lashes curled back, shaking with sobs, she looked up at the face bending over her. She might have thought she had died and gone to heaven if it hadn't been for the sheer physical pain of coming back to life. Only living could hurt this much.

'You're going to be OK,' Max said quietly.

Her throat was raw; slowly, painfully, she managed to whisper, 'How did...? I was in the sea...how did I get here?'

'I saw you and swam out to tow you in.'

She was stunned. 'In that sea?' Behind her she could hear its roar, the thunder of the waves hitting rocks. The very sound of it made her shiver.

'I'm a strong swimmer.' His voice was curt, dismissive.

'You could have been drowned,' she said, eyes stinging with tears.

He shrugged. 'As I said, I'm a strong swimmer, and I know these waters. I often swim off this beach. If I hadn't gone in, you *would* have drowned—you were going down for the last time when I reached you. I was afraid I wouldn't reach you in time.'

110

She was seeing him through running curtains of water—at first she thought they were her tears, then she realised rain was pelting down.

'You saved my life. Thank you.' Every word cost her an effort, her throat was so swollen and sore.

She started violently as lightning tore down the sky. It seemed to be right overhead, the whole landscape lit up: boiling dark sea, banked clouds in the sky, a lone pine tree bending and swaying on the rocky cliffs above the beach.

Max got to his feet. 'We'd better get you indoors.' He bent and slid his hands underneath her, one under her knees, the other under her back, and lifted her as he straightened.

'I can walk,' she protested, too weak to struggle.

'Put your arms round my neck; it will make it easier for me,' was his only response to that.

Her arms felt heavy as lead as she lifted them; it was a relief to let them fall over his shoulders, clasping her trembling hands behind his nape.

Max began to walk quickly, with her held close to his body, her legs dangling, her wet, bedraggled skirts clinging against her sides. His clothes were saturated too, his shirt plastered to his chest.

'Where are we?' Olivia's voice was just a hoarse whisper, like the wind through dry, winter grass.

He looked down at her in obvious surprise. 'Hymnos—where else?'

'How far... to your house?' She remembered being told that there was a long walk up a steep track, and got out thickly, 'You can't carry me all that way.'

'I'm not going to. I drove down here. How else could I get here fast enough? I saw you from the cliff top, saw

you fall off the yacht, and I got into my Land Rover
and drove down here like a bat out of hell.'

He lifted his head and stared away into the night, and
she watched his profile tense, tighten.

'I thought I wouldn't get here in time,' he muttered.

Olivia hadn't dared hope anyone would get to her in
time. 'There was nobody on deck. I don't suppose anyone saw me fall in...' She frowned weakly, biting her
lip. 'They won't know...until the morning when they
find my cabin empty. Haven't you got radio equipment
here? You could send a message to the yacht, let them
know I'm safe.'

'I could,' Max said in a dry voice, and when she looked
up at his profile it was set, unreadable. He wouldn't want
to talk to his half-brother, of course, or her father, and
who could blame him?

She sighed, and then felt her heavy lids closing. She
couldn't force them up again. She drifted into semi-
consciousness, too weary to fight the exhaustion taking
her over.

Dimly, she was aware when Max put her into the back
of his vehicle, laid her down full length, heaped blankets
on her, got behind the wheel and began driving up the
rutted track to the house.

Olivia was jolted and shaken every inch of the way,
but she lay under her blankets, trembling, her teeth
chattering with cold and shock. She didn't try to sit up
or look out. She kept her eyes shut, even though she
had recovered consciousness.

The vehicle stopped with a little bump, then Max
got out and came round to get her out. First he wrapped
her in one of the blankets, then lifted her bodily over
his shoulder in a fireman's lift, her head hanging
down behind him.

A door opened; yellow light shone round her, penetrating her closed lids. She opened her eyes then and blinked at the radiance, trying to see past it to catch a glimpse of the house, but Max had already begun to carry her inside.

He closed the door and the storm receded at once. Olivia stared around her and saw white walls, a greeny-white marble floor, a polished oak staircase leading upwards.

'First, a hot bath,' Max said, carrying her up the stairs.

She thought of it longingly; her very bones were aching with cold. She couldn't wait to slide into the warmth of a bath, wash the salt off her skin, out of her hair.

Max sat her on a wicker bathroom stool and turned to the large white bath; she heard the water gushing out. Her brain wasn't working very fast, but she suddenly stiffened.

'I can manage by myself now,' she hurriedly said, and Max straightened and looked round at her, his eyes ironic, his mouth wry.

'You can hardly move.'

It was true. She was half-dead from her long struggle with the sea, but she insisted, flustered at the very idea of him staying in the room while she took a bath.

'I can manage. Please, just...' She didn't like to finish the request. He had risked his life to save her, this was his home. She didn't like to say, Go, get out, I don't want you watching me take off my clothes.

'I don't want you drowning in my bath after I've pulled you out of the sea!' he said, sprinkling scented bath salts into the water. The bathroom filled with the fragrance of roses.

'I'm fine now,' she lied.

Max turned, surveyed her sardonically. 'OK, then, let's see you standing on your feet.'

She managed it, struggling up, gripping the edge of the bath to keep herself upright.

'There, you see?' she said, eyes defiant.

'Oh, yes, I see,' he drawled, walking towards her.

Alarmed, she backed, had to let go of the bath, and swayed dangerously. Max's arms went round her, stopping her from falling.

'Don't be so stupid,' he told her. 'You aren't even capable of unzipping your dress at the moment.' His hand moved up her back, she felt the long zip slide down, and thought, He's right, I couldn't have reached the zip, it's hard enough to do it when I'm feeling fit, but my arms are so heavy and tired. Every movement is an effort.

Max peeled the wet, clinging material off her body and the dress slithered to the floor. She felt him start to push the straps of her slip down over her arms.

Flushed and nervous, Olivia babbled, 'No, don't, that's enough...'

She tried to shift away but his arm was an iron bar across her back. His dark eyes held hers while he very slowly slid her slip down over her breasts, her waist, her hips, until it too fell to the floor.

Mesmerised, staring deep into his eyes, Olivia stopped trying to get away, gave herself up to the intense pleasure of feeling him look at her, touch her. She had had dreams like this—dreams she only dimly remembered—where Max touched her, naked, kissed her. In her waking moments she wouldn't let herself remember, but now the dream emerged into the light, was really happening, wasn't a fantasy, and she trembled and couldn't breathe.

He unclipped her bra, let it fall, and then she felt the slow, warm brush of his fingertips on her breast; her nipples hardened, rosy-pink and stinging with sensation.

'Max...don't...you mustn't,' she whispered.

He looked into her eyes. 'Tell me you don't want me to....Tell me you don't like it...'

His hand travelled on, stroking over her midriff; he slid it inside her wet silky panties and she gave a little moan.

'I can't.'

'Can't tell me you don't like it?'

'Can't let you do it!'

'You can stop me if you tell me you don't like it,' he whispered.

The panties had gone; she was naked and he was looking down at her body in a way that made her skin hot, unbearably hot.

'Don't look at me like that!' She turned her face into Max's wet shirt, shuddering.

His hand covered the back of her head; he stroked her hair, lowered his cheek against it, murmuring inaudibly.

All she could hear was her own name. 'Olivia...Olivia...'

His other hand stroked down her body, her shoulders, her back, the soft swell of her buttocks; she felt pulses begin to beat everywhere he touched.

Suddenly he picked her up in his arms and she gasped, looking up at him. He was staring down at her body, the dark glitter of his eyes half veiled by their lids, his lips parted, his breathing audible, rapid. Suddenly he bent and kissed her breasts, his mouth opening over her nipples, sucking them in, his tongue caressing them.

Olivia felt a pleasure so sharp it was like a sword thrust into her. A groan forced its way out of her throat, even though she tried to keep quiet, not show him how he made her feel.

Max lifted his head, his skin dark red and burning hot. He looked into her eyes and his mouth went crooked as he tried to smile.

'I want you like hell, you know that, don't you?'

Olivia couldn't get a word out. She looked away, blushing, trembling.

A second later Max dropped her into the bath. She gave a choked cry; water went sloshing everywhere in a tidal wave. Max stood there laughing as it went over his legs and bare feet.

'Look what you've done... You're crazy!' she stammered. The marble bathroom floor was awash with water.

Max undid his shirt and flung it off. Olivia felt her nerves jump. 'What are you doing?'

He kicked his jeans off. 'What does it look as if I'm doing?'

'You aren't getting in here with me!'

'Yes, I am.'

She didn't know what to do. She couldn't get up again, try to get out of the bath; the cloudy, fragrant water was at least some sort of cover for her nakedness.

Out of the corner of her eye she saw that he was naked now, the strong, brown body moving towards the bath. Her heart almost stopped; she wanted to stare, to see all of him and at the same time she couldn't bear to look. She kept her head averted, but even so she saw one long, tanned leg stepping into the water, followed by another. Her eyes shot upwards, then down again, her face scarlet.

'I was in that sea too. I'm frozen to the marrow,' Max said, sinking into the water up to his chin. He closed his eyes and sighed deeply. 'Oh, that's better.'

His legs touched hers, one on either side of her. Olivia was stiff with awareness, feeling the muscled thighs moving against her. She stared at his face, so familiar yet so unknown, alien, puzzling.

With his lids down he looked like a blind statue: eyeless, formidable, carved stone features, a strong nose, tough cheekbones, jawline that threatened, a mouth which made her throat beat with a hot pulse.

His lids rose and he stared back at her. She didn't know what he was thinking. Worse, she was afraid of what he might be thinking.

Her colour rose higher. She wanted to look away but couldn't, wanted to ask him to go away, get out of the bath, leave her alone, but she couldn't say a word.

He shifted his position; his thighs moved in closer to her, enclosed her firmly, rubbing softly against her. She knew what she would see if she looked down into the bath: their flesh, clearly visible through the water, entangled together.

'You mustn't forget to wash your hair,' Max said, and got up, dripping, a golden-brown statue, very male. She thought he was getting out of the bath, but he reached for a shower attachment on the wall, and a moment later stood over her, directing it down on her head.

'I can do it!' Olivia sat up, water running down her face, and tried to grab the shower head from him, but he moved it away, turned it off, opened a cupboard above the bath and got out a bottle of shampoo.

'Let me do it!' said Olivia, but he ignored her. He tipped a creamy liquid into his palm, knelt down and began rubbing it into her hair, kneeling in front of her, his strong fingers massaging her scalp. Olivia shut her eyes, as much to stop herself seeing Max naked as to protect her eyes from trickling soap bubbles. He rinsed the shampoo off, then repeated the process.

'Dry your hair,' he ordered, tossing her a clean, dry towel.

She obeyed, conscious of him watching the graceful lift of her breasts as she towelled her hair. Max was shampooing his own hair.

'Chuck me the towel if you've finished,' he said, and Olivia leaned over to hand it to him. As he began to dry his hair she stood up, intending to get out of the bath.

'Where do you think you're going?' Max asked, dropping the towel on the floor. He caught her by the waist and pulled her back into the water, this time lying on top of him, her body between his parted legs.

All the air seemed to be driven out of her lungs.

'Don't, Max,' she whispered, feeling his hands sliding over her bare flesh, his chest behind her back, his body moving against hers.

'You didn't use any soap; there must still be salt on your skin,' he huskily murmured, his chin on her shoulder, his lips moving against her ear.

He picked up a bar of soap and began washing her slowly, rhythmically, methodically: first her shoulders, her arms, then softly over her breasts, while she trembled, closing her eyes. The firm hand moved on down and Olivia cried out.

'Oh...' It wasn't so much a protest as a response, an instinctive, mindless response to unbearable pleasure.

She had never slept with anyone; no man had ever touched her there before. It was the most secret, the most guarded, the most sensitive part of her body, and as Max's fingers invaded it she shook violently.

'No!' she muttered, very flushed, pushing his hand away.

Max didn't argue. Instead, he closed his hands on her waist, lifted her, spun her round, lowered her again, the breath catching in her throat as she found herself looking into his eyes.

He began soaping her back, her buttocks, her legs in that slow, exploratory fashion while he watched her face.

'You really turn me on, Olivia,' he whispered, then he lifted his sleek, dark, seal's head from the bathwater until their mouths met.

He turned *her* on; she couldn't deny it, even to herself. She kissed him back hungrily, her blood singing in her ears, giving in to the urge which had gripped her ever since she saw him taking off his clothes. She had never touched a man like this before; she and Christos weren't lovers—their kisses were affectionate rather than passionate, and there was no desire between them. She realised with a flash of understanding that there never would be, could be; she believed Christos was fond of her, and she was very fond of him, but he was more like a brother than a lover.

What hope had there ever been of her falling for any other man when she had belonged to Max, body and soul, ever since they met on that beach in Corfu? He had spoilt her for other men. None of them ever matched up. There was no one like him. She didn't want anyone else.

But she wanted him. She wanted him so badly she felt sick. She touched him with shaky hands, caressed his broad shoulders, the deep, muscled chest, ran her stroking fingers downwards and heard Max draw a long, sharp breath.

In their excitement they forgot where they were, their bodies tangled, shifting eagerly, coming closer, sliding down deeper into the water.

It was only when the bathwater came up over their faces that they broke apart, spluttering, laughing.

'The water's getting cold,' Max said, his voice thick, husky. 'Time to get out.'

He got out first and watched her rise from the water, her skin glistening, pink and wet. Max handed her a long, fluffy white towelling robe, shrugged into an identical one, and helped her tie the belt of hers around her waist.

'I'll go and find us a hot drink and something to eat,' he said. 'You get into bed.' He gestured out of the steamy bathroom, across the landing into a spacious, carpeted bedroom. A vast, four-poster bed took up the centre of the room; gauzy lace curtains hung around it.

'We don't have much trouble with mosquitoes indoors now, so long as you never open the shutters after dark, because these days we plug in electric insect killers every night,' Max said, as Olivia stared at the bed curtains. 'But when the house was first built, I did get pestered by mosquitoes, so I had these curtains installed round the bed, and slept behind them every night. I don't have to bother now.'

He pulled the curtains back. 'In you get. You need to keep warm. You're probably still suffering from shock.'

'I don't want to take your room—there must be others,' she protested, not meeting his eyes.

Max turned down the silky amber-coloured duvet cover. 'Get in my bed, Olivia.'

She knew then that he meant to share the bed with her.

'I can't sleep with you!' she wailed. 'I'm engaged to Christos, I gave him my word.'

Max took hold of her waist and almost threw her into the bed, pulled the duvet cover over her, and gave her a dark stare.

'You're not with him now. You're here, with me. I saved you from drowning—if it weren't for me you would be dead now. That makes you mine. I saved your life, so it belongs to me.'

She clutched the duvet, staring back wordlessly, her ears deafened by the sound of her beating blood.

Max turned and went out. For a minute she was frozen, then she rolled off the bed and almost fell over. Shaking, she made it to the door, to lock it and shut him out.

There was no lock or bolt on the door.

She quietly opened it and stood listening; she heard Max moving about downstairs, presumably in the kitchen. Olivia looked along the landing at the other doors. If any of those rooms had bolts or locks on the doors she could lock herself in and keep Max at bay until morning. She ran to the nearest door, opened it, saw at once that it had neither bolt nor lock, ran on to the next and found the same.

Why didn't he have locks on the doors?

Why bother on an uninhabited island? she realised. Who would he be locking doors against? But what if he had uninvited visitors? Criminals intending to burgle the house, or even kidnap or attack him? She was amazed that that shouldn't worry him.

She heard him then, coming up the stairs, and ran back to the main bedroom, climbed into the bed, clutching the white towelling robe around her, and pulled the duvet up to her chin and lay, waiting anxiously, her heart pounding right under her ribs.

Her eye caught something high up on the ceiling at the other side of the room. A little red light pulsed there, with a black box suspended on a pivot. What on earth...? Then it dawned on her.

A security system! So that was why Max didn't bother with locks or bolts. He had some sort of electronic security system installed here. If anyone broke in while he was here, an alarm would go off. What if he wasn't here, though? Ah, but then what use would locks and bolts be if there was nobody here, nobody to hear someone breaking down the door, smashing windows? No bolt or lock could keep out a criminal determined to break in. The only purpose of the alarm was to give Max warning, time to prepare his defences.

Then she looked at the camera again and blushed to her hairline, appalled. Was it on now? Had it been filming her? Was there a camera in the bathroom too?

Max came through the door at that moment, carrying a tray; the scent of coffee, of food, filled her nostrils and she suddenly felt hungry, which was ridiculous because she had had dinner not that long ago, but then so much had happened since then. Tension used up all your energy; her blood sugar was probably very low.

'Is that camera up there working?' she asked Max, who looked round over his shoulder at it, pausing mid-step.

'No, it isn't switched on.'

'There's a red light.'

'That is nothing to do with the camera—it means the security system has been switched on and nobody can get in or out of the house without setting off an alarm. The windows are alarmed, so are the exterior doors, and the stairs. I just set it before coming up here. It wasn't on five minutes ago.'

'But the camera isn't on?'

He shook his head. 'I only set that when the house is empty, to film any intruders.'

She watched him, hoping he was telling the truth. She thought he was; Max had a direct stare that made him very believable.

'Is there a camera in the bathroom?' she asked and Max gave her a dry, amused look.

'No.'

'Honestly?'

'Go and look, if you don't believe me! Now, are you hungry?'

'Well . . . I had dinner on board, at . . .' She lifted her arm to look at her watch.

She wasn't wearing a watch any more. It must have come off in the sea, she thought, the strap had been loose. Her father was going to be furious! That watch had been a Rolex, one of his birthday presents, and had no doubt cost a fortune.

She didn't look forward to telling Gerald. Her golden eyes darkened at the thought of her father.

'Have you been in touch with the yacht yet?' she asked Max as he set the tray down on one side of the bed.

He gave her one of his hard, narrowed stares. 'I'll do that later. If they think you're in your cabin they won't start worrying until morning, as you said.' He poured coffee from the silver Georgian coffee-pot which matched the silver tray it stood on, and offered her a cup.

Olivia reached for it and at that instant realised something else, staring at her left hand dumbly without taking the coffee.

'Oh! Oh, no . . .' she groaned. It was bare. Her engagement ring had gone. That, too, must be washing about in the sea. It must have come off, like her watch, while she was fighting to swim ashore. She had noticed only the other day that it was very slightly too big for her and had meant to take it to a jeweller to have it altered to fit better. She knew she had lost weight over the last months, since her engagement began, in fact; that was why both ring and watch no longer fitted the way they once had.

'What's the matter now?' frowned Max.

'My ring... I've lost my engagement ring. It must have come off in the sea.'

He stared at her in silence for a moment, then said, 'Do you believe in omens, Olivia?'

'No!' she denied, but she was lying. She did. It might be a coincidence that she had lost her ring tonight. But Olivia couldn't help feeling that it was a very odd coincidence, happening at precisely this moment, when she was about to find herself isolated on this island with Max and faced with the temptation of his lovemaking. A ring was only a symbol of an engagement; losing it didn't mean she was free and yet she couldn't pretend it made no difference. It was as if fate had intervened to make it easier for her to forget about Christos and her promise to marry him.

'I do,' said Max in a deep voice. 'Now, drink your coffee, Olivia, and eat one of these.'

She took her cup of coffee and stared at the plate he had laid on the cover in front of her. She recognised pitta bread, the flat, mostly unleavened Greek bread which could be toasted and split to hold food. The smell of grilled lamb was delicious; she flapped back the split pitta and saw salad with the pieces of lamb kebab it held, rings of onion, chopped lettuce, tomato and cucumber.

'I shouldn't eat any more,' she told him, her mouth watering at the smell of the food, scented with thyme and rosemary and lemon.

'I've cooked it now; you might eat it,' Max said, sitting down on the end of the bed and taking a bite of his own pitta sandwich. 'Mmm...it's delicious!'

She ate some too. He was right, it was delicious.

'Did you grill it over charcoal?'

He nodded. 'Most of my cooking is done over charcoal, and I tossed the salad in lemon and a little natural yoghurt.' He grinned at her. 'I'm a good cook, if a little limited. I cook either fish or meat when I'm here—the lamb's my own. I run a few sheep here, and goats, keep some meat in deep freeze for when I'm here, but I mostly live on fish. I enjoy fishing off my yacht—the snapper is very good around here, so is the mullet, and I catch lobster, prawns, squid and sardines, clean them and gut them, sprinkle them with herbs and a little lemon juice, and chuck them on to the barbecue, serve them with some plain boiled rice or salad—a quick, simple meal and very healthy.'

Olivia had finished her sandwich. She thirstily drank some coffee; it was strong and very good. She was on edge, nerves prickling. How was she going to stop him getting into bed with her? He knew now that she wanted him, she hadn't been able to hide it. He wasn't going to be stopped by the fact that she had promised to marry another man, especially as the other man was his nephew. Christos might not be the man who had snatched Max's company away from him, but she had no doubt that in Max's eyes he shared his father's guilt.

Somehow she had to bring the temperature down, make this crackle of electricity between them die away.

Huskily, she asked, 'When you aren't here, who looks after your animals?'

Max answered casually enough, smiling at her. 'A fisherman and his wife come over several times a week, check that everything is OK. When I'm here, they sometimes stay to help out; it is a useful addition to his income, especially if the fish aren't running. A bad fishing trip can mean hard times for them. They're glad of a guaranteed second income. In weather like this they can't get over, of course. It takes them a couple of hours to sail here.'

'So it takes them all day to sail here and back again?'

'They usually stay overnight—there's a staff flat over the garage. Then they sail back next day, unless there are urgent jobs to be done, and then they stay longer.'

Max took her plate and cup, put them on to a table near the window, and came back, untying the belt of his white towelling robe.

Her heart racing, Olivia said hoarsely, 'Max, I'm not sleeping with you! I'm still engaged to Christos...'

'Tell me you love him,' Max said, letting his robe fall to the floor, and her golden eyes opened wide, pupils dilated with desire, riveted on him, her mouth going dry. He was so beautiful; she wanted him so fiercely.

She swallowed. She couldn't lie to him, with those jet eyes fixed on her, watching every expression passing through her face.

'I am engaged to him!' was all she could say.

'But you aren't in love with him and never have been.'

She bit her lip, colour coming and going.

Max pulled back the duvet and she shrank against the pillows. 'No, Max! Don't.'

'Why did you get engaged to him when you didn't love him?' he asked, his hand reaching for the belt of her own robe.

She grabbed his hand, pushing it away. 'I'm fond of Christos—it seemed a good idea.'

He laughed harshly. 'A good idea? You mean your father pushed you into it, and his father pushed him— they're using you, both of you, ruthlessly. Your marriage is the cement in the unholy alliance between my half-brother and your father. They don't trust each other, with good reason, so they've each offered up a child, as a hostage for good behaviour.' He looked into her eyes. 'That's the truth, isn't it, Olivia? And you know it.'

She sat there, her face white suddenly, stricken, nodding. She hadn't faced it before, but she knew, had always known, from the moment she met Christos and realised that her father wanted her to date him, that it had all been set up. She was being manipulated towards an arranged marriage.

'How could you let your father do that to you?' Max asked as though he despised her for it, and she couldn't answer; tears welled up into her eyes and trickled down her cheeks.

'Did you want his approval that badly?' Max asked, and she found her voice, even though it shook, answered that, wildly, tears running down her face now.

'Maybe I did... I suppose I did... I've always been scared of him, all my life, ever since I was little. He's always been there, like one of those Easter Island statues, on my horizon—never making sense, never human, staring over my head, stony, cold, faraway. He has never once shown me affection, do you know that? I suppose I wanted him to; I wanted him to be pleased with me, just for once. I wanted him to look at me and see me, really see me, smile at me. Don't we always want our parents' approval? Is that so odd? OK, I knew he and Constantine were pushing me and Christos at each other, and I'm sure Christos knew, although we never talked about it. One half of me knew it wasn't what I wanted, that I didn't love Christos and never could, but there was that other half which got in the way. I knew my father wanted me to marry Christos, and I wanted to please him, so I let it happen.' She was white, sobbing, she looked angrily at him. 'You have no right to despise me for it, anyway, it's none of your business!'

Max got into bed with her and pulled her, struggling, into his arms, gentling her as if she were a panic-stricken animal. 'Ssh . . . I'm sorry, don't cry like that, ssh . . .' He stroked her hair and Olivia lay against him, her crying slowly dying away until she was still, soothed into sleepy warmth.

'I'm so tired,' she whispered. 'I just want to go to sleep, Max.'

'Go to sleep, then,' he softly said, holding her, and she gave a long sigh, her body relaxing against him as sleep swallowed her up.

When she woke up again, the first thing she saw was light on the opposite wall—it was morning. The second thing to hit her was that she was now naked; at some time during the night Max had taken off her robe. She hadn't even been aware of it going, she had been sleeping too deeply.

Max lay behind her, breathing rhythmically in sleep, his warm, naked body touching hers from shoulder to knee. Olivia lay awake, listening to him, crazily happy to feel their close contact. They lay together like spoons in a drawer, fitting perfectly together, as if they belonged like that.

She wished she could see him, but dared not risk moving, for fear of waking him up. The physical effort of swimming against the currents to tow her in to shore must have been enormous; he must be as tired as she had been last night. Rested, she felt much better now, although her throat still ached; she was wryly afraid it would hurt for days. But at least she was alive, and so was Max. It could so easily have gone the other way; she could be washing around in the sea like her watch and her ring.

Involuntarily she was wrenched by a deep sigh, and Max shifted and yawned. Olivia froze. Was he waking up? She gave a gasp as his hands softly moved upward and touched her breasts.

'Good morning,' he whispered, his lips on her bare shoulder. 'You slept well—how do you feel?'

'Fine,' she muttered, pushing his exploring hands down, her breathing very audible. 'Don't, Max.'

A second later she was on her back and he was arching over her, looking down at her with smouldering, demanding eyes.

'I spent most of the night watching you and fighting with the urge to make love to you while you couldn't argue about it,' he bit out. 'But you were so tired I let you go on sleeping. We're both wide awake now though, and you aren't a schoolgirl any more, Olivia, you're an adult woman. It's time you started facing facts. We both know what we want and how we feel. You never loved Christos, your engagement doesn't mean a thing, does it?'

Her lips shakily parted; he put a fingertip on them, silencing her.

'Ssh . . . no more talking, Olivia. Let's just make love.'

CHAPTER SEVEN

OLIVIA felt hot tension coil inside her stomach; she wanted him, wanted him so much it hurt. But she turned her head away, talking fast, her voice shaking. 'No, I can't, Max, please understand—not while I'm engaged to Christos. I must tell him first, you've got to see that. OK, I'm not in love with him, any more than he's in love with me, but I am fond of him, and I did say I would marry him. Until I've broken off my engagement, I can't...just can't...'

'Don't be ridiculous!' he burst out, his voice thick with frustration. 'You admitted last night...your engagement doesn't mean anything.'

'It means I said I'd marry Christos, so I'm not free,' she muttered.

Max caught her head between his hands, forcing her to look at him, his black eyes fixed and fierce.

'You are going to break it off, though? You're going to tell Christos?'

His stare was hypnotic. 'As soon as I get him alone,' she whispered.

'Your father isn't going to like it,' he warned, and she almost laughed at the understatement.

'No, he isn't.' She didn't look forward to telling her father. She knew how he would look at her, how his cold eyes would make her feel.

Max watched her, his brows black and heavy. 'I'm afraid of his influence over you, Olivia. He isn't going to accept it—and he and Constantine will try to make you marry Christos.'

'They can't *make* me!' she said, whistling in the dark, desperately hoping she was going to be strong enough to stand against their anger.

Max's voice was harsh. 'Oh, I'm not talking about actual bodily force. They won't make you go through a marriage ceremony at gun-point, but there are other ways of forcing someone to do what you want. You've admitted that you got engaged because your father wanted you to.'

'Yes, but he didn't force me to get engaged! I just knew he would be pleased if I agreed to marry Christos.'

Max's mouth twisted. 'Oh, come on, Olivia, we both know your father scares you. You're so eager to placate him you'll do whatever he wants.'

She flinched at the very idea of her father's fury when he heard she wasn't going to marry Christos, but she had made up her mind.

'Not this time,' she said, and Max watched her, his face hard.

'All the same, I think it would be safer to present them with a *fait accompli*. If you and I were lovers there'd be no more talk of making you marry Christos. I know the men of my family—he would never marry you once you'd slept with me.' He smiled cynically. 'Oh, I'm not saying he'd insist on you being a virgin, not these days, but the idea of you sleeping with his own uncle... No, he wouldn't stand for that.'

Olivia stiffened, ice trickling down her back. Was that why he wanted to make love to her? To stop her marrying his nephew? Did he really want her, or was she just a weapon in his war against his brother and her father? Was he using her to get revenge? After all, he hadn't bothered to get in touch with her all these years—she might never have forgotten him after they met in Corfu, but Max had never tried to see her. No doubt he'd forgotten she existed—why kid herself? After all, why should he remember a schoolgirl he'd spent just one day with?

For her it had been different. That one brief meeting had made a deep, indelible impression on her. She had never forgotten him, even though she tried.

Had she betrayed herself, that day when he'd walked into her father's office in a black mood, the day they got control of his company? She had been so stunned to see him. Those vibrations of fierce attraction had begun again, and she hadn't been able to stop them. Had he picked them up? Had she somehow betrayed herself? Had he realised she was vulnerable to him?

Max read her changing expressions and frowned. 'What's wrong? What are you thinking? Say something, don't just look at me like that.'

He was doing it again, tuning into her mind, picking up what she was feeling and thinking, even when she tried to hide it from him.

Pain and then anger grew inside her. She put her hands flat on his shoulders and shoved, violently.

She caught him off guard. He sprawled backwards on the bed and Olivia quickly slid down from it to the floor, saw her white robe lying across a chair and grabbed it, hurriedly wrapping herself in it with trembling fingers as Max sat up and stared at her.

Once she was covered up again, she felt much safer. Of course, he was a powerful man, much bigger than she was, and much stronger, and they were quite alone here. If he chose to try force... But he wouldn't, she thought quickly. Not Max. She was certain of that, but still very edgy, because all her senses were so aware of him, naked on the bed, the golden skin gleaming in the morning sunlight. His body riveted her eyes—strong shoulders, a deep, powerful chest, his legs long and muscular.

She swallowed, desire hot inside her. She tied the belt of her robe tighter, one hand pulling the lapels of her robe across her breasts and throat.

'I'm not sleeping with you, Max!'

'We'll see about that,' he said in a soft voice that made her pulses beat fiercely.

'Are you threatening rape?' she angrily asked, and he frowned.

'That isn't funny, Olivia.'

'It wasn't meant to be. You'd have to use rape because I mean what I say. I will not sleep with you.'

'Listen——' he began, but she interrupted, a flush growing in her face.

'No, I won't listen! I'm sick of being pushed around, I'm sick of living my life to please other people. From now on, I'm going to please myself. I'm not giving in to anybody, not my father, not your brother, or Christos, or you!'

Max's eyes had narrowed, hard and watchful. For a moment he didn't move or answer her, then he said curtly, 'Keep thinking like that! Because you're going to be under a lot of pressure to go through with that marriage—have you got the backbone to stand up to your father and keep saying no, Olivia?'

'Yes,' she said, without a flicker of doubt this time. She couldn't say to him, I'm so angry with you that I'm no longer afraid of my father. I don't care what he thinks or how he talks to me. Her golden eyes said it though, glowing with the deep smouldering rage of the lioness.

'I wonder!' Max got off the bed and Olivia tensed, took several steps backwards.

'I meant what I said!' she warned again, and was given a long, dry, level look.

'I very much hope so.' He picked up his own robe, which lay on the floor, and slid into it, turning towards the fitted wardrobes which ran all along one wall of the room. 'Now what am I going to find you to wear? You can't put that chiffon dress back on, but none of my clothes is likely to fit you. I'm a head taller, for one thing, and built very differently.' He gave her a hard grin, then slid back one of the wardrobe doors, revealing neatly hung rows of clothes, most sheathed in covers. Max clicked through a line of jeans and cotton shorts, immaculately ironed shirts, then stopped and pulled down a large, baggy cotton sweater, which he threw to her. 'This is very long—could you wear it as a dress?'

She caught it and held it away from her to assess it. 'I think that would work. Thank you. I'd like to have a shower before I try it on though.' Her voice faltered. 'I...I suppose my...my other clothes are still wet?'

'Your bra and slip?' he said drily. 'No, they must be dry by now. While I was waiting for the coffee to percolate last night, I rinsed them out, to get the salt out of them, and hung them on the heated towel rail in the bathroom.'

Her face was startled. 'Thanks,' she said again. 'That was very thoughtful.' She wasn't used to being looked after by a man; most men she knew tried to get out of doing any household chores, and she would never have suspected Max of being the domesticated type. He was the most male man she had ever met, big and tough and with far too much machismo.

If she had thought about it though, she might have worked it out. After all, he lived here alone, sometimes for weeks on end, with only occasional help from the fisherman and his wife who looked after the property when Max wasn't here. She should have realised Max had to be very practical and quite self-sufficient, able to attempt any chore around the house, not needing other people's company, or he wouldn't choose an uninhabited island as his favourite retreat.

What did she really know about him though? She hardly knew him at all; yet she always felt she did. There had been an instant sense of familiarity, almost of recognition, the moment they'd met. Maybe she was kidding herself, maybe it was all illusion, but whenever they were together the same sensation returned: a sense of belonging, a warmth and security. She might not know everything about him—but a deep, inner conviction told her that the details of his character, his likes and dislikes, his hopes and fears, didn't matter as much as that instinctive, intuitive sense of belonging.

If she ever got the chance, she would be able to fit the pieces of the jigsaw which was Max Agathios together, finding out if they shared the same taste in films, music, books, places, food. If they didn't it wouldn't be important—they were two separate people; she didn't expect them to be mirror images of each other. All that truly mattered was the way he made her feel, and that was something she had known on sight the first time they met, even though she had been so young, even though she had never been in love before.

Because that was the truth, wasn't it? She was in love with Max, and she had been in love with him for five long years.

The sound of his voice, so familiar, so important to her, startled her out of her reverie. 'You can use the bathroom we used last night.'

She looked dazedly at him.

'Are you listening, Olivia?' he asked, coming closer, and her heart turned over inside her.

Somehow she nodded and said, 'Yes ... of course ...'

'Hmm ...' he said on a doubtful note. 'Well, I'll have my shower in the bathroom across the landing, then we'll have breakfast. I'm expecting Spiro and his wife later today—the couple who look after the place while I'm away. They're coming over to get the house in shape before the auction. They were coming yesterday, but when the auction was postponed I sent them a message to come a day later.'

She remembered his brother's irritation on getting the news that the auction was postponed, and that in turn reminded her that she must let them know she was safe. Urgently she said, 'You won't forget to get in touch with the yacht after you've had your shower, will you?'

He looked at a clock on his bedside table. 'Ten past eight,' he said. 'I expect Constantine will be up by now; he always gets up early. He's such an obsessive character that he works long hours, even when he's supposed to be on holiday. The question is, when will they start wondering why you haven't appeared?'

'I don't know, not yet maybe, but I don't want them to think I've drowned—please get in touch at once.' Her golden eyes pleaded with him.

'After I've showered and dressed,' he said curtly. He collected clothes from the wardrobe and a chest of drawers, and went out without giving her another glance. He had not been pleased to be asked to contact his brother's yacht.

He would enjoy knowing that they all believed she
was dead, thought Olivia with a pang of dismay. Max
had called his half-brother obsessive—but what was he?
They were driven, both of them, possessed by hatred of
each other.

Sighing, she made her way to the bathroom they had
used last night. It was spotless again—Max had tidied
away the towels they had used, and the bath was
gleaming. He was a very surprising man.

There was no lock on the door, so she moved a chair
that was in the room into a position in front of the door,
propped up below the handle. It wouldn't keep Max out
if he was determined to get in, but it would at least delay
him long enough to give her warning. She hung up the
white robe, turned on the shower and stepped under it,
hurriedly washing her hair and then herself. She wanted
to get dressed as soon as possible. She would feel safer.

When she had towelled herself dry, she put on the bra,
slip and panties she had found, as Max had promised,
on the heated towel rail, and then lifted his white cotton
sweater over her head.

The sleeves were too long; she had to roll them up or
they would have hung down well below her hands. It
could certainly pass for a dress, although it ended before
knee level. It was baggy, but then that was quite
fashionable, and the material was finely woven, soft thin
cotton which clung where it touched, especially over her
small, high breasts and the soft curve of her hips.

She eyed herself in the mirror doubtfully. Actually, it
looked rather sexy, she realised, taken aback by her reflection. She hadn't expected that. She had thought she
would simply look absurd, but the deep V of the neckline
showed the plunge of pale, smooth breasts, and the
hemline revealed far too much of her thighs. The effect

of the dress was distinctly provocative, and Olivia wasn't happy about wearing it.

Max hadn't offered her any alternatives, though, and she certainly couldn't put her green chiffon evening dress on again, so it would have to do.

Sighing, she found a hairbrush among the toiletries on the bathroom shelves and slowly brushed her short blonde hair, wishing she had some make-up with her. Her face was pink and shiny from the shower. She looked schoolgirlish—until you noticed the way the sweater clung, she thought, mouth wry.

As she left the bathroom she walked straight into Max, who steadied her with both hands on her shoulders.

'Well, well,' he murmured, looking her over slowly. 'It suits you—you should always wear my clothes.'

Pink, she tried to change the subject. 'I'm starving—did you say something about breakfast?'

He laughed, his dark eyes glinting with mockery at her confusion. 'Yes, you can help me make it.'

She hadn't noticed much about the ground floor of the house last night, but now she looked around with curiosity at the hall they entered at the bottom of the stairs. She remembered the white walls, the marble floor which was streaked with green, but the pictures hadn't impinged on her last night. She took them in now: big seascapes and landscapes, blue and white and green, full of light and space. They covered the walls to the back of the house. On each side she saw doors leading into other rooms, caught glimpses of shining floors, light golden oak furniture, pale walls.

'When will you radio the yacht?' she asked, and got a sideways glance from Max.

'As soon as we've had breakfast.'

He pushed open a door and they walked into the kitchen, which was large and full of sunshine—the storm had blown itself out now, she saw, looking out of the window into a garden full of trees and shrubs. The grass was littered though, with leaves and branches, with torn flowers and a few tiles which must have been blown off the roof of the house.

'It was a really bad storm, wasn't it?' she murmured and Max nodded.

'I wouldn't have liked to be out at sea last night. I hope Constantine's captain rode out the storm in the bay. We'll be able to see the yacht from the headland—we'll drive up there later. There's a rough track. The four-wheel-drive takes it easily enough.'

He put on the coffee, asking her, 'What do you want for breakfast? How about scrambled eggs?' and when she nodded added, 'Will you scramble them while I lay the table?'

While she melted a small piece of butter on the hob, beat eggs and poured them into the pan, Max squeezed oranges, cut some slices from a loaf of domed Greek bread and laid the kitchen table. Just before the eggs were ready he produced a bowl of field mushrooms, cleaned and ready to cook, put a pan on the hob next to the one she was using and began to fry the mushrooms rapidly with some sliced tomato.

They ate breakfast side by side in front of the garden window. The coffee was as strong as it had been last night, and just as delicious, especially after the fresh, tangy orange juice and the food.

Max leaned back in his chair, eyes half closed, his expression contented.

'That was the best breakfast I've eaten for years.'

'Yes,' Olivia agreed, feeling far more alive now. 'Is your food brought over by your fisherman?'

'Some of it. Some I bring over in my boat, and the mushrooms I picked myself.'

She gave him a startled look, rather worried by that. 'You did? Picked them here?'

'Yes, some of them among the pines up there behind the house. A lot of mushrooms like the sandy soil in pine woods, did you know that? It's a good place to look for mushrooms—and they like birch trees too.'

'Are you an expert?' she nervously asked. 'I mean . . . you are sure those mushrooms were edible?'

He grinned at her. 'Don't worry. Of course, you have to be sure you know which are safe to eat and which aren't; it's easy to make a mistake and pick a poisonous mushroom which looks like an edible one. I have an illustrated book which shows the differences very clearly. I check any I'm not certain about.'

'I hope you were certain about all those we ate!' she said, laughing a little uneasily.

Max turned his dark head to smile at her lazily. 'Tell me if you start to feel ill, if you begin to throw up and everything goes black before your eyes!'

'Is that a symptom of mushroom poisoning?' she asked, worried.

'Well, it's certainly a symptom of something!' teased Max.

She made a face at him. 'Very funny. Will you get in touch with the yacht now? Christos may be banging on my cabin door at this very moment.'

He shrugged, untroubled by that. 'Knowing my nephew, I'd doubt that; he is not an early riser. I think they'll wait until nine to start banging on your door. So let's clear the table first, and load the dishwasher.' He got up and began collecting up the plates. 'I have every possible labour-saving device here—and the best available electric generator to keep them all working! I try to be self-sufficient.'

'So that you don't need anybody,' Olivia said quietly, getting up too, and he gave her a quick, penetrating glance.

'I told you, I do have people to come in and clean the house thoroughly every few days, and look after the livestock, especially if I'm not here.'

'But you don't need people,' said Olivia. 'You're self-sufficient; you prefer your own company. That's why you have a yacht you can sail single-handed, and a holiday home on an uninhabited island. You like being alone—you don't really like people enough to want them around much.'

He considered her, his black eyes hard and narrowed, his face unyielding. 'Amateur psychology, Olivia?'

She was putting the cups and plates into the dishwasher; straightening, she gave him a cool shrug.

'Just guesswork.'

'Hit-and-miss guesswork, Olivia,' he said drily. 'Oh, it's true, I like being alone—but it doesn't really follow that I don't like other people. I like some, I don't like others. I have plenty of friends, not to mention colleagues I like and trust. But if you're really talking about my half-brother, then no, I don't like or trust him, with good reason, as you know perfectly well. He has always hated me, from the day I was born. He resented my very existence. He wanted to be my father's only son. Of course, he hated my mother too, and made her life a misery. When he heard my father's will read out and discovered that I'd been left this island and some ships, he was so angry I thought he was going to kill me there and then. He coveted everything my father left me, and he was determined to get it all away from me. I knew that. I was always on my guard, but in business you have to take risks if you want to get anywhere. I had to borrow large sums of money to build up my company— how could I have guessed Leon would die so suddenly, and leave me wide open to attack? I had a run of bad luck—first a rise in interest rates, and a fall in business, then one of my ships sank, but none of that would have mattered if it hadn't been for Leon's death. That was my real blow.'

She watched his dark eyes, seeing the pain in them. 'You were really fond of him,' she realised, and Max gave her a bleak look.

'He was a close friend, a second father, he believed in me and I trusted him absolutely. You don't often meet someone like Leon. I'll never meet his like again, I'm sure of that. Losing my company isn't as heavy a blow as losing Leon.'

She bit her lip. 'How will you feel if Constantine buys the island at the auction?'

Max gave a mimicry of a smile, his teeth bared in a movement more like a snarl.

'How do you think I'll feel?'

Her nerves leapt. 'You won't like it,' she whispered, and he laughed then, angrily.

'You're so English, Olivia. Strong emotions terrify you, don't they? What you want is nice, bland, safe feelings; you're like a ship that never leaves harbour in case it meets strong winds or hits a rock. Doesn't it ever occur to you that, comfortable though your secure little harbour may seem, you're never going to experience any of the elation or excitement that comes with taking risks?'

'No, but I'm not going to drown either,' she said huskily.

'You're a coward,' he muttered, mouth crooked.

Olivia lifted her chin, defiance in her golden eyes. 'Not any more. I told you, I'm going to face up to my father.'

'And life? Will you face up to that? I wonder.' His mouth was crooked with angry mockery. 'I can't see you leaving your safe harbour and risking yourself on the high sea, can you?'

She thought of the great, greeny-black waves that she had had to fight her way through last night, the agony of trying to swim against overwhelming forces, the moment when she realised she was going to drown. Her face turned white.

Max was watching her intently, his eyes hypnotic, terrifying. She felt the force of his will, felt her body weaken, trembling, felt her senses drown in passion.

He took a step nearer and her pulses leapt. 'Don't touch me!' she cried out.

'Why not? It's what you want, what we both want,' he said huskily, and his hand reached for her, closing round her nape, his fingers strong and warm. 'The minute I first saw you, I knew I wanted you,' he said, and she wished she could deny that it had happened to her as instantly, but she knew he could feel the fierce racing of her pulse under his fingertips.

It made her angry to know she couldn't hide her reactions; she looked up at him, her golden eyes bitter.

'It couldn't have meant much—I never heard from you again, after that day! You forgot I existed.'

His eyes flashed, violence flaring in his face. 'That isn't true! I've never forgotten you—but I couldn't get in touch with you. I'd given your father my word.'

She froze, incredulity in her face. 'My father? What do you mean?'

'That night in Corfu, when we got back from sailing to Paki, he said you were much too young to know what you were doing. He didn't want you getting romantically involved with anyone yet, he didn't want you distracted from your studies, he wanted you to go on to university and get a degree. What he was afraid of was that you would throw up everything else to get married, and waste your brains. He told me he wouldn't give his permission for me to see you, and neither would your mother. She was even more determined to see you go to university, he told me. She believed in careers for women; she was against early marriages.'

'That's true, she is,' admitted Olivia. 'More than my father, in fact; I thought he just went along with the idea of further education for me because my mother insisted on it.'

'Well, he convinced me. I didn't want to be responsible for you giving up your chance at university; education is far too important. He made out a good case—said that we had only just met, one day wasn't enough for either of us to be sure it was going to mean anything, and it wouldn't be fair of me to try to grab you before you had had a chance to grow up, look around, find out about yourself.'

She looked at him tensely—what was he saying? That he had been as attracted to her as she had been to him?

'He asked me to give him my word I wouldn't try and see you again,' Max said flatly. 'At least, not until you left university.'

Olivia was stunned. 'He never told me!' Her face tightened with anger as she realised just what her father had done.

Max grimaced. 'He's quite a psychologist, your father. He knew me well enough to realise I'd listen to his plea to leave you alone until you were at least twenty-one. He pointed out that I was a lot older, and I'd met a lot of other women. He wanted you to be free to experiment, find out about yourself, meet other men. He asked me to wait. He said that as we often see each other at board meetings, he'd keep me in touch with what you were doing. I always asked after you—he told me you were working hard, and although he thought you often had dates, there was nobody special in your life.'

Flushed, she murmured, 'He was telling the truth—there wasn't.'

Max looked at her, his eyes hard, glittering. 'Not even Christos? He told me months ago that you were going to marry Christos.'

She looked at him sharply. 'Months ago?'

'Some time in May. I saw him at a board meeting and asked if you were going to spend your summer with him as usual, and that was when he told me you were going to marry Christos.'

Slowly, Olivia said, 'I only met Christos for the first time this summer, in Monaco. We didn't get engaged until just before the end of the holiday.'

They stared at each other. Max said something in Greek under his breath; she didn't understand the words but it sounded like swearing.

'He lied,' she said, almost incredulously because it was so outrageous a lie, so unbelievable.

'Yes,' Max said through his teeth. 'He was determined to keep us apart.'

'He knew I hadn't forgotten you,' she recognised, looking back over the last five years, and her eyes darkened. 'How could he do it?' Then, bewildered, 'Why did he do it? Deliberately, for his own ends, lying to stop you seeing me again, plotting to get me to marry Christos, when he knew I...' She broke off and Max looked down at her quickly.

'When he knew what, Olivia?' he whispered, and her colour deepened to wild rose. Max moved closer, brushed her hot cheeks with his fingertips as if to check that the colour was real.

'I wasn't deluding myself five years ago, was I? You felt it too, and I think your father picked it up at once.'

'How could he?' she broke out, her voice shaking with anger. 'How could he do that to me?'

'He hates me,' Max drily said. 'I'm not sure why. I've never done him an injury. I can't think of a single reason why he should dislike me so much that he'd lie and cheat to keep me away from his daughter.'

Uncertainly, Olivia said, 'He said you had a reputation, there had been a lot of women in your life, you were a playboy.'

Max laughed angrily. 'A playboy? He has an old-fashioned vocabulary, your father. That makes me sound like something in a 1950s B movie! I worked too damn hard for that—but I can't deny I like women. I'd dated quite a few over the years, but somehow it always fizzled out, it never turned serious. None of them was what I knew I wanted.'

Her whole body trembled with hope, with passion, with tenderness, then she remembered something else and her face tightened again.

'He also told me you were going to marry Leon Kera's daughter.'

Max shot her a frowning glance and grimaced. 'Yes...that wasn't actually a lie. We weren't formally engaged, but we had been seeing each other that year, quite a lot, and I was beginning to think Daphne might be the one...' He broke off, shrugging, and Olivia felt a sting of jealousy—had he and Daphne Kera been lovers? Was that why Daphne had been so bitter that she had sold her shares to Constantine?

'When I got back from Corfu I stopped seeing her,' Max said. 'I had to tell her why, of course.'

Olivia waited, breathless.

Max's face was grim. 'Daphne was bitter about it. I can't blame her. She knew as well as I did that I had been thinking of marrying her, even if nothing had been said. Her father wanted it, and I was very fond of Leon. If I hadn't met you, I would probably have married her, and we would both have been unhappy once it dawned on us that we'd made a mistake. I was very glad when Daphne met her big Australian because I could see she was going to be happy with him.'

'But she went ahead and sold her shares to your brother,' Olivia said quietly. 'If she's happy, why would she want to ruin your life?'

Max was silent for a minute, his dark face shuttered. In a bleak, flat voice, he said, 'I hurt her. I knew I had, I wished I hadn't, but I had to, once I'd met you. I couldn't marry Daphne then. But she took after her father in many ways—she had tunnel vision, she always went after what she wanted with unshakeable tenacity and she never forgot an injury. The fact that she was happily married to someone else didn't stop her being determined to have her revenge on me for the hurt I'd inflicted five years ago.'

Olivia couldn't help feeling sorry for Daphne, in spite of what she had done. Her bitterness was such a clear indication of how much Max had hurt her. Yet how could she go so far in her desire to hurt him back? She had wrecked his life.

'I wonder how she feels now,' she thought aloud. 'When she thinks about what she's done to you.'

Max laughed shortly. 'Pleased with herself, no doubt, for having got her own back. Daphne is a tough woman.' He gave Olivia a look which held laughter, tenderness. 'Unlike you.'

'I don't want to be that tough,' she retorted. 'I'd hate myself.'

'I wouldn't like you much either,' Max said, eyes amused, then he sobered. 'What I really can't fathom is why your father has always disliked me so much that he was determined to stop me seeing you.'

She sighed. 'I think he always wanted to be a big tycoon, get seriously rich, but he never quite made it, because he's far too cautious. He's like me, he doesn't take risks, and it seems to me that unless you take risks you don't make spectacular gains. He inherited a solid company, and he has run it well, but he has never really achieved all he dreamed of in the beginning. You've already made more of a name for yourself than he ever has—and my father can't forgive you for being what he wanted to be.'

Max's brows had risen as she talked soberly. 'You see him pretty clearly, don't you? I wonder if that's it. Maybe. I know he's full of seething envy and ambition. It doesn't seem much of a reason for trying to force his own daughter into marrying someone she doesn't love, does it?'

'I don't think he cares a damn what happens to me. I doubt if it ever occurred to him to think about my feelings. All he wanted was a chance to hurt you, in any way he could. That I might get hurt in the process was never important.'

Max put his arms round her and pulled her close, her face buried in his shirt. He stroked her hair and murmured huskily into her ear, 'He won't hurt you any more, I promise you that. He'll have me to deal with in future.'

She leaned on him, her eyes closed, feeling his warmth percolating through her, secure in his strength.

Somewhere in the house a clock chimed and her eyes flew open. 'It's nine o'clock! We were going to radio the yacht at nine...'

Max let go of her, his face wry. 'Yes, I suppose we have to let them know you're safe, although it would serve them right if we didn't bother.'

'I may be angry with my father, but he is still my father. I wouldn't want him to think I was dead,' she said gently. 'And then there's Christos... We aren't in love, but I'm fond of him. I'm sure he's fond of me, he'd be upset if he thought I'd drowned, and...'

'All right, all right,' Max said, winding his arm around her waist. 'You've made your point. We'll do it now.'

They walked back through the house and into a sunlit room furnished as an office with a leather-topped desk taking up the centre of the floor, one wall lined with locked filing cabinets and bookcases, against the opposite wall a fax machine and a photocopier, against another a desk occupied by expensive radio equipment.

Max sat down in front of the radio and began flicking switches while Olivia watched, fascinated. 'I'm putting out my call sign,' he said, and then stopped as an urgent voice came out of the speaker, talking in Greek.

Olivia didn't understand what was being said, and watched Max's face intently, anxiously, as he answered.

His expression had changed; he was frowning, she was sure his skin had paled, and his voice sounded harsh, disturbed. He spoke quickly, tersely, in muttered Greek.

After a very brief exchange, he switched off and sat there for a minute staring at nothing, his head bent.

'What is it?' Olivia burst out, tense with anxiety.

He looked around at her, his black eyes all pupil. For a minute she almost thought he wasn't seeing her, then his eyes focused and he gave a deep sigh.

'I'm sorry, I'm afraid I have bad news for you. There's no easy way of telling you this—the yacht has been trying to get in touch with me for some time, it seems. At eight o'clock this morning your father knocked on your door, and when he didn't get a reply he went in and discovered you weren't there and your bed hadn't been slept in. He raised the alarm, the yacht was searched, but of course there was no sign of you. Then they realised that you must have gone overboard during the storm. When the captain told your father, he had a heart attack.'

CHAPTER EIGHT

OLIVIA was still in shock when Max drove her down to the little stone-walled jetty where the yacht would tie up when it arrived. By then they could already see the yacht sailing towards them at full speed, the white prow cutting through the waves and sending a line of white foam curling back along the hull. The sea had calmed since last night; in fact it was like a millpond, vivid blue with the sunlight dancing over it and making a mosaic of little glittering facets; and the sky was so bright that the light blinded Olivia. She had to shield her eyes as she watched the yacht's approach.

'Where is that helicopter?' she fretted, looking up at the empty skies. 'Didn't you say it would arrive before the yacht got here? Why isn't it here yet? The sooner he gets to hospital, the better chance he's got. If there's any delay...' Her voice quivered and she broke off, then after a minute said, 'He never mentioned having a heart condition—I'm sure he's never had a heart attack before. I thought he was so healthy, and he isn't even sixty yet—that isn't very old.'

Max put an arm round her shoulders, his hand gripping her upper arm. 'Stop it! Don't work yourself up into another crying jag. You mustn't start worrying.'

'How can I help it? It's all my fault...'

'Olivia, for heaven's sake!'

'It is! If——'

'Don't start another of those sentences that begin with "if"! You didn't deliberately throw yourself overboard, did you? You fell off the boat by accident—how can it be your fault your father had a heart attack when he heard you were missing?'

She obstinately finished the sentence he had interrupted. 'If we'd got in touch with the yacht earlier he wouldn't have thought I had drowned and he wouldn't have had a heart attack!'

'That was my decision,' he said curtly. 'If you want to blame somebody, blame me.'

There was a silence. She did, and they both knew it. Her golden eyes darkened with accusation and grief as she looked up into his watchful face.

Her voice was husky, low, angry. 'We should have let them know I was safe.'

His face tightened as if she had hit him. 'OK, I should have got in touch earlier than I did, but I had no idea he had a heart, let alone a heart condition!'

Her skin lost every touch of colour, so white that her lips looked almost red although she was wearing no make-up. 'How can you say such a cruel thing when he could be dy——?'

'He isn't going to die!' Max exploded and she felt the tension in his body, in the arm which held her close to him, in the hand biting into her upper arm. 'How many times do I have to tell you—I didn't get the impression this was a very serious heart attack.'

She wanted to believe him, but she was afraid to be too optimistic. 'You can't be certain about that!' she muttered, trying to pull out of his grip.

Max refused to let her go; his arm tightened even more, holding her closer, but when he answered his voice was gentle.

'Olivia, if I'd had any idea that this might happen I'd have got on to the yacht last night. I deliberately delayed getting in touch because I thought it would do your father good to have a shock. I thought...well, I suppose I hoped that if he believed you were dead he might realise how little he'd ever valued you. It might start him thinking about you, make him see how he'd been treating you, using you, pushing you into a marriage which was just one of convenience—his convenience, not yours!'

The yacht was very close now; they heard voices on deck, saw faces staring down at them, but Olivia was so stunned by what Max had just said that she didn't try to distinguish one face from another. She looked away, and angrily asked Max, 'Why didn't you tell me why you weren't in a hurry to get on the radio?'

'What would you have said if I had?' he asked in a dry tone, his mouth twisting.

'I'd have insisted you talk to them at once!'

Max laughed shortly. 'That's what I thought. I guessed you would be horrified by the idea of scaring him into taking a long, hard look at himself and his relationship with you, so I didn't bother to say anything to you.'

'You had no right to play God at my expense!'

'Maybe not, but I was only thinking of you. I had the best intentions.'

She gave him a bitter look. 'Are you sure you were thinking of me? Are you sure you weren't just getting your revenge because my father had helped your brother snatch your company away? Maybe you see his heart attack as karmic justice!'

His eyes flashed, his skin darkened with fierce blood. 'Is that what you think?' he harshly asked, letting go of her, his hand dropping to his side. His stare was hostile, piercing. 'Thanks very much.'

He strode angrily away from her to the end of the jetty as the yacht slowly backed into place, the engines almost at a standstill now, making very little sound, and at that instant the sky filled with the noise of a helicopter arriving.

Olivia fought with her tears, her throat salty with them, relieved to be able to concentrate on the helicopter, following its progress towards the helicopter pad near the house, on the high ground overlooking this bay. The olive and cypress trees stirred, whipped to and fro, bending almost to earth, the silvery-green leaves of the olive and the dark flames of the cypress agitated into a frenzy in the wind of the propellers as the machine settled down between them.

Even Olivia's blonde hair was wind-blown, tumbled about her pale face in light, ruffled waves.

Max swung round and walked rapidly back, his face rigid, jet eyes as sharp as knives.

He hates me! she thought, her stomach sinking as if she were in a lift which suddenly dropped like a stone. But her own anger was still fierce enough for her to stare back at him unsmilingly. If he had got on the radio last night, her father would never have had this heart attack.

Through clenched teeth Max bit out, 'I'll drive back up there at once, to pick up the doctor. You wait here—when they come ashore, tell them I won't be long, and they had better wait until the doctor gets here before moving your father.'

She nodded without speaking, unable to risk opening her mouth for fear she might break down altogether.

Max gave her another hard, angry look, and stalked away. She heard him start the vehicle, heard it roar away, but kept her eyes fixed on the yacht manoeuvring closer to the stone wall of the jetty. There was barely room for the large vessel to tie up—the jetty was very small and narrow, meant to take only small boats, like Max's own yacht, for which a special boathouse had been built nearby. From where Olivia stood she could see the white blur of the boat in the shadowy interior. No doubt Max had sailed here from Piraeus, like themselves.

Someone stared down at her from the deck of the *Agathios Athena*. She looked back, pale and tense, at Christos. She had never seen him look so serious; his tanned face was tight with control, his dark eyes searching her own face, as if looking for evidence of what had happened to her since they last saw each other.

The gangway was let down, locked into position and Christos walked to the head of it, but before he could descend his father had pushed past him and begun coming down towards her.

She felt her nerves leap as Constantine's bull head lowered, as if he were about to charge, his sullen eyes surveying her suspiciously, morosely, accusingly.

'How's my father?' she broke out huskily.

'Very ill,' he grated. 'Did you spend the night here?'

Her face burned. 'Didn't Max tell you? Yes, he rescued me, I was drowning and he swam out to save my life——'

'Who else is in the house?' demanded Constantine. 'Are those people who work for him here?'

She shook her head, aware of Christos coming up behind his father, watching her over his broad shoulder, his face shuttered and unreadable.

'You were alone here with him all night?' Constantine asked through lips that were tight with rage.

'I want to see my father,' she said. 'I'm going on board——'

'Not until you've answered me,' Constantine ground out, the whites of his eyes yellow with rage, little flecks of red around the pupil. 'Where did you sleep? Where did he sleep?'

She was trembling violently. 'Can I see my father, please?' she said again.

Christos said flatly, 'Let her go and see her father, Dad, stop hassling her—can't you see she's too upset to talk?'

Constantine turned to glare at him. 'I want the truth out of her, but she won't tell me anything. What do you think that means? It's obvious, isn't it? He's had her, and she doesn't want to admit it—she knows what will happen if she does. You aren't going to marry her after she's slept with him, are you?'

Olivia almost threw up, sickened and humiliated by his crudeness.

Christos looked uneasily at her white face and darkened eyes. 'I'm sorry, Olivia, but can't you set his mind at rest? Tell him nothing happened, and he'll leave you alone!'

She heard an intake of breath nearby, looked up and was appalled to see a row of faces on the deck of the yacht. The crew were all leaning on the rail, watching them and listening avidly.

In a low, shaking mutter, she said, 'I'll discuss it when we haven't got an audience!'

Both men looked round and up, frowning. Constantine's dark red colour deepened even more; he glared and bellowed, 'Get back to your work, all of you!' and his crew vanished hurriedly.

Olivia said quietly, 'On second thoughts, ask Max your questions, not me!'

Constantine glowered at her. 'Oh, I will, don't worry! If I get the chance! I notice he vanished as soon as I arrived!'

'He went to pick up the doctor from the helicopter,' she retorted. 'He'll be back. Oh, and he said you weren't to move my father until he got back.' Olivia paused, swallowed, and asked tersely, 'Now can I go and see my father? Was it a very bad heart attack?'

'It isn't so serious as we thought it might be at first,' Christos said in a gentler tone. 'We talked on the radio with the doctor who has flown out here—he's a heart specialist from the nearest mainland hospital, and he gave us advice on how to treat him. He's conscious and stable, but we must get him to a hospital as soon as possible.' He paused, frowned, and said slowly, 'You know, maybe you shouldn't see him, Olivia, not yet, not until the doctor is here. The shock of seeing you might bring on another attack.'

'Haven't you told him yet that I'm alive?' she broke out, appalled.

'Yes, of course, as soon as we heard it ourselves, but if you talk to him he might start asking questions, and the next you know he'll be working himself up into a state, the way my father just did.'

'He knows Max, he knows how far he'd go to hit back at us,' Constantine said heavily.

'Yes,' Christos said in grim tones, and they both stared at Olivia, who gave them a stricken look. She thought how close she had come to letting Max have sex with her last night, and felt a wave of nausea rise up inside her. What if Christos and his father were right? What if Max had taken an opportunistic chance of revenge on them? After all, she and Max had only met twice before—five years ago they had spent one whole day together, but then they hadn't met again until a few weeks ago, when he had come to her father's office and confronted her angrily.

What did she know about him? How had he got so close to her so quickly that she had been on the edge of giving in to him last night?

From the rough track leading up to Max's house came the sound of the four-wheel-drive vehicle bouncing over the ruts and stones towards them.

Olivia sighed with a strange sort of pain, and with relief. Max was coming; just knowing that she would see him again in a minute hurt and was a wild, sweet pleasure all at the same time. Her emotions were so confused, entangled, where he was concerned.

Thank God, though, he had the doctor with him. She could see other people in the vehicle—her father would get medical attention at last, and must soon be on his way to a hospital, for which she was deeply relieved and grateful.

Constantine glowered along the track, scowling. 'I'll get some answers now, if I have to smash the truth out of him! I intend to know exactly what happened here last night.'

'I almost died, that was what happened!' Olivia muttered angrily. 'And he saved my life. Not many people would have tried, in that sea—the waves were huge... I thought I had no chance... I was drowning, going down for the last time, but he swam out there and towed me in. I'd swallowed so much sea-water he had to pump it out of me.'

'God, you must have been scared stiff,' said Christos, looking and sounding as if he really cared. She had shaken him; his skin was almost as pale as hers. 'I don't know if I'd have had the nerve to swim out there in that storm. Oh, come on, Dad, whatever happened after that, it was very brave of him—and at least Olivia is alive! I don't know about you but I'm very grateful for that.'

Constantine gave him a contemptuous look, but didn't answer. Olivia couldn't stop a choked little giggle, which made him glare at her.

'Your father would rather I were dead!' she muttered, and Christos looked shocked.

'Of course he wouldn't, Olivia! He's just upset.'

A moment later, Max's vehicle screeched to a stop and a short, thin man wearing a white coat over a suit, followed by a nurse in a blue uniform, climbed out. 'Where's the patient?' the man demanded in a thick-accented English.

'Are you Dr Kariavis? The patient's still on the yacht—we were told not to move him until you came!' Constantine snapped, his heavy-lidded eyes glancing at his half-brother and away again as if he couldn't even bear to see Max.

'Well, I'm here, so let's get on board. There's no time to waste—the sooner I see him, the better,' the doctor said.

He walked towards the gangway, a large black case in one hand, and Constantine followed, talking to him in a rough, impatient mutter in Greek.

Olivia began to follow, but Christos caught her arm. 'Better wait until the doctor has seen your father, he'll advise us whether or not he's well enough to talk to you.'

Max watched them both, his body as taut as a bowstring, his face tense and grim.

Crew members came off the yacht and helped get a stretcher out of the back of Max's Land Rover. They carried the stretcher up the gangway, the nurse bringing up the rear with some other equipment which the medical team had obviously also brought with them in the helicopter. Max helped her carry the heavier items.

Christos touched her arm and she glanced up at him.
'Now that my father's not here, tell me what really happened?' he coaxed. 'Olivia, we're engaged. Don't you think I have the right to know what went on last night? I know Max has been interested in you for years——'

'What? What do you mean?' she asked sharply, eyes widening.

Christos looked sheepish, hesitated, muttered, 'Dad told me ages ago, before I even met you.'

'Told you what?' she repeated.

He shrugged. 'Oh...that Max had met you and fancied you, but that your father had warned him off because you were still at school.'

'My father told him.'

Christos nodded.

Rage mounted to her head. Her father had talked to Constantine, but he hadn't told her, had deliberately kept Max's interest in her a secret, as if she had no right to know something that important! Her father had treated her like a child! Then she thought, Well, at least he had some excuse—I was his child, he had known me all my life and was used to making decisions for me without consulting me. What about the way Max had behaved last night? He treated me like a child too; and he had no such excuse. I'm not his child, I'm a grown woman, yet he decided not to let my father know I was safe and deliberately didn't tell me what he was doing, or why. It's unforgivable.

How dare they treat me like this, both of them? She wanted to hit them, scream and yell at them, let her anger out.

But she didn't; she fought with it, refusing to let her
mind cloud with all that red smoke of rage. She needed
to be clear-headed, needed to think.

'How long ago did your father start plotting with
mine?' she asked Christos, who looked wary.

'My father's never liked Max, you know that,' he
hedged.

She looked into his eyes. 'They ordered you to propose
to me, didn't they?'

Christos took on a faintly shifty look, and went red.
'They didn't order... Well, Dad did say something about
it being a good idea, but... well, I knew I'd get married
some time, have a family. I wanted children. And I had
no one else in mind. I'm very fond of you... We get
on, don't we? We had a lot of fun in Monaco. I wouldn't
have proposed if I didn't like you.'

'Did they bribe or threaten?'

'Neither!'

'You know we aren't in love, Christos,' she said. 'You
proposed because they told you to!'

He took on a sulky look; he began moving his foot
drawing circles on the sand which last night's storm had
blown all over the jetty, staring down at what he was
doing as though absorbed in nothing else.

'What's he been saying?' he muttered. 'You're dif
ferent. I'm beginning to wonder if Dad's so far wrong.
Something did happen last night, didn't it? He's been
talking to you, putting ideas into your head.' He looked
up, his lower lip sullen, his eyes accusing. 'For heaven's
sake, Olivia, can't you see that he's using you to get his
own back on us? He may fancy you, but he wants re
venge too, and this way he could kill two birds with one
stone—sleep with you and at the same time hit back a

us for pushing him out of his company! He's a snaky bastard, you can't trust him an inch.'

She couldn't help laughing at that, but her eyes were angry. 'I certainly can't trust you, can I? Or your father? Or mine, come to that. You all plotted against me. You were only marrying me because it was a good business arrangement—it was my father's company you were marrying, not me, only you didn't bother to explain that. I was being sold a romantic deal, not a business contract, which was what it really was! It was all phoney, and you were in on the plan. I wasn't, was I? I was the only one who didn't know what was really going on!'

Christos burst out, 'That isn't fair, Olivia! I never plotted against you. I really thought we'd be happy together, I was serious about our marriage. OK, it wasn't exactly a love match...'

She laughed again, even angrier.

He gave her a furious look, even his ears red. 'Arranged marriages often work out better in the long run...'

'Who says so? Your father?'

'Yes, OK, he does, but I think he's right about that. You fall out of love. I know that. I've been in love several times—it never lasts, and then you get nasty squabbles and bad feelings left over. It was different with you and me. I thought we were friends. I was sure it would work between us.'

'Without love?' She shook her head, her eyes sombre. 'You know that isn't true. Liking isn't enough, Christos. I'm sorry, I do like you, and I thought we were friends too, but I got stampeded into our engagement, and I realised almost at once that I couldn't go through with it. Max didn't need to tell me anything I hadn't worked out for myself. I'm afraid I lost my ring last night in the storm. I can't give it back to you. It is insured, though, isn't it?'

'Yes,' he said curtly. 'I'll deal with the claim.' Then, 'He won't marry you, you know,' he muttered. 'Not after what your father did to him. He hates your family too much to marry into it.'

She was wrung by a spasm of fierce agony. He was right, of course. Max would not want to marry the daughter of a man who had tried to destroy him. There was no future for them.

She heard movements and looked round quickly. The crew were slowly, carefully, making their way down to the jetty again, carrying the stretcher, with her father strapped on to it.

Max was hurrying ahead. He passed her and Christos without so much as looking at either of them, and opened the back of his vehicle so that the stretcher could be slid inside without difficulty. The back seats had already been let down flat, leaving plenty of room.

Olivia met the crew as they reached the jetty. Her father's grey face was covered with an oxygen mask, but he was conscious; he looked at her, his hand stirring weakly on the blanket covering him.

She bent to kiss him on the cheek.

'You're going to be OK, Dad.'

Tears showed in his eyes and she saw his throat move, as if he was trying to speak to her. She read the wordless question in his face.

'I'm fine, I'm sorry you were worried. Don't try to talk, Dad, save your strength,' she said, horrified by the way he looked. He had aged ten years at least; all the life had been bled out of him overnight. Suddenly he looked old.

She held his hand tightly.

'Can I go with him in the helicopter?' she asked the doctor as he briskly came towards them, his white coat flapping in the wind blowing off the blue sea.

'I'm sorry, there won't be room.'

She turned pleading eyes to Max. 'Couldn't I squeeze in somewhere? I'm not very big.'

'It will be crowded as it is. The stretcher will take up a lot of room,' Max curtly said.

'We'll take you on the yacht,' Christos promised. 'But we can't leave until after the auction.'

Max's black brows jerked together. 'No need,' he said through his teeth. 'My helicopter will be back as soon as they've delivered him to the hospital.'

She looked down at her father. 'I'll follow as soon as I can,' she promised, kissed him again and stood back so that they could slide the stretcher into the back of Max's vehicle.

Max climbed behind the wheel and set off at a slow, steady pace. Olivia saw Constantine coming down the gangplank and looked up at Christos.

'I don't want to talk to your father, he'll only try to bully or browbeat me. I'll leave it to you to tell him that the engagement is over. I'm going to walk up to the house and wait for the helicopter to come back for me.'

She set off without waiting for Christos to reply. There was nothing else to be said now—she hoped she would never see either of them again.

Constantine called after her angrily, but she didn't look back. She kept going up the steep track, aware that Christos was talking to his father, and then that they were both following her, their feet scuffing in the dust, grating on the rocks underneath.

It was not an easy climb; she was soon out of breath and behind her she heard Constantine panting in thick gulps.

'Dad, do you want to have a heart attack too?' she heard Christos say anxiously. 'Take it easy! Why don't you sit down on that boulder...take a rest for a while...? Look, here comes Max again...he can give you a lift up to the house.'

Max's Land Rover drew up beside Olivia. He leaned over to open the door on the passenger side, looked at her grimly.

'Why didn't you wait on the jetty?'

'You'd better pick up Constantine, he'll never make it to the top by himself.'

'Get in,' he said through tight lips. 'I didn't invite him to my house—he can go back to his yacht.'

'He won't. He'll just have a heart attack trying to walk up to your house.'

'That's his problem, not mine. Get in!'

'You can't let your half-brother kill himself.'

'Why not? It would save me the trouble of doing it.'

She looked scathingly at him. 'You're as bad as he is! The two of you need your heads knocked together!'

Max switched off the engine, put on the brake, and got out. As he walked around the vehicle she began to hurry on upwards, but he caught her before she had gone half a dozen steps. He picked her up bodily, ignoring her squawk of protest, the muttered, 'Max, put me down!' walked back to the Land Rover and deposited her ungently into the passenger seat, then slammed the door on her before she could try to get out again.

Christos and Constantine caught up with them before Max had got back behind the steering-wheel.

'Go back to your yacht,' Max told them. 'The auction is off and I don't want either of you in my house.'

'Off?' roared Constantine.

'What do you mean, off?' Christos chimed in, his voice almost drowned by his father's.

'I've cancelled it; the island isn't for sale any more,' Max said brusquely. 'I'd like your yacht to leave immediately. This is private property, and you're trespassing.'

Olivia watched them in the driving mirror. Constantine was scarlet with exertion and heat, breathing thickly, glaring at his half-brother.

'When did you call it off?' he panted. 'Just now, after putting Faulton on to that helicopter? Oh, don't think you can pull the wool over my eyes! I know what you've been up to. You think you've been very clever, don't you? You've managed to break up my son's engagement, and Faulton's had a heart attack because you deliberately didn't let us know the girl was safe with you— if he dies, and she inherits, you'll marry her for her shares in your company, so that you can get me off the board of your company again.'

'If you don't cool down, it will be you having the heart attack, from the look of you!' Max drily said. 'Goodbye, Constantine. See you in the boardroom very soon.'

He climbed behind the wheel and started the engine again. Before he drove off, Christos materialised at the open window on Olivia's side.

'Remember, whatever he says, he's used you to get his company back, Olivia,' he said bleakly. 'You can't trust him.'

CHAPTER NINE

'COULD she trust *you*?' Max asked, and drove off with a grind of tyres on rock, a roar of the engine.

In spite of the mounting heat of the day Olivia felt cold and weary; she sank back in her seat, staring out of the window at the gleam of sunlight on olive trees, the dark shade of pines and cypress lying in pools beneath them. Beside her Max was silent, yet she felt his attention as she glanced sideways at his brown hands manipulating the wheel without effort.

The way he had manipulated her, she thought bitterly. Effortlessly, without even needing to try. Those hands had touched her and she had been lost. She despised herself. She had been a coward where her father was concerned, and a fool over Max.

'Do you think you're going to get your company back now?' she asked, and Max flicked his dark lashes towards her, his face guarded.

'Probably.'

Her mouth was bitter. 'Now that my father is a broken man and I'm not going to marry Christos any more, you mean?'

The lashes lifted; she caught a glimpse of those glittering, furious black eyes, then they were hidden again, but his face was clenched tight with rage.

'Be careful, Olivia!' he said through his teeth. 'Don't push your luck!'

'Luck!' she repeated, laughing scornfully. 'I haven't had any—not as far as men are concerned, at least. First

Christos proposing just because his father wanted him to—and then you...'

He pulled up outside the house with a grinding of gears and turned to confront her, his dark face tense and dangerous. Her pulses went out of control and panic made her tremble violently, but she put her chin up and defied him.

'Don't you come anywhere near me!'

'What will happen if I do?' he mocked angrily, sliding along the seat until he almost touched her. 'Going to beat me up, are you? My knees are knocking—can you hear them?'

'Oh, you think you're so funny!' she fumed, moving back even further until she was right up against the door and had nowhere else to go. 'I've got news for you. You aren't funny—I'm not laughing. Just because I'm a woman and not as strong as you are, you think I'm a pushover, don't you? You think you can make me do whatever you want. You, my father, Christos—you all treat me as if I was a halfwit, without a will of my own. Well, listen to this—I mean what I say! I don't want you touching me. Have you got that? I don't want you touching me, Max. I'm saying no, and I mean it. If you try to force me——'

'Did I try last night?' he bit out and she stiffened at the harsh tone. 'I had you naked in my bed, in my arms—and we were alone, miles from anyone else. I could have forced you then, Olivia, but I didn't, did I?'

She stared back at him, remembering the night before, biting her lip. It was true. He hadn't really argued that hard, he had accepted her refusal, even though she knew very well he hadn't wanted to—his frustration had been far too evident.

'I can't think straight,' she muttered. 'My mind's shot to pieces. I don't know what to believe. All I can think about is that my father may die...' She stopped short, gasped. 'My mother! I ought to have let her know he's been taken ill.'

'I thought they were divorced?'

'They are, but they were married; she'll be upset to hear about his heart attack. Can I phone her from here? I could have rung from the yacht; it never occurred to me.'

'You can phone from here.' Max opened his door and jumped down. Olivia got out too, before he came round to her side of the Land Rover.

She looked up at the empty blue sky. 'How long will it take the helicopter to fly to the mainland and come back for me?'

He looked at his watch. 'The pilot promised to turn right round at once—I'd say he'd be back here in around an hour.'

An hour alone with him! she thought, trying to control the rapid beat of her pulse, the hectic flow of colour in her face, aware of Max watching her intently, monitoring her reactions, his dark eyes narrowed and hard and dangerously bright. He was picking up too much, he was too clever; she was afraid of those sharp eyes of his, that even sharper mind.

She walked on ahead, too quickly, and pushed open the front door of the house, only to have it swing back on her as she was walking through it, the edge of the door striking her shoulder.

She gave a little squeak of pain and surprise, clutching her shoulder.

'What have you done to yourself now?' Max sounded furious and she resented it.

'Nothing! Can I ring my mother at once, please?'

'In a minute. Show me where that door hit you first.'

'I'll do nothing of the kind! I tell you, it was nothing, just a glancing blow, it doesn't hurt.'

Well, not much, she thought, aware of the throbbing pain on the soft pad of her shoulder.

'Then why is there blood on your sleeve?' asked Max, and she quickly looked down sideways, startled.

'I must have broken the skin—grazed it a little, it can't be anything much. I'll look at it later, after I've rung my mother.'

'You'll let me look at it now,' Max insisted again. 'If the skin is broken and you're bleeding that could be dangerous if it isn't dealt with at once, out here. You never know what you could pick up in an open wound. I'll wash it and put some disinfectant on it, put a plaster on it until you can get a doctor to look at it. When did you last have a tetanus shot?'

'Within the last six months.' She hesitated, then began rolling up her sleeve. Maybe he was right—she should let him put a plaster on the shoulder.

'No, that won't do—get the whole sweater off,' Max said.

Flushed and breathless, she opened her mouth to protest, and he gave her an impatient look.

'And don't turn coy on me! If you were on a beach you would think nothing of wearing a bikini in front of dozens of men. I've seen you naked and I've seen you in your bra and panties before, so just get my sweater off and stop arguing.'

'You're doing it again!' she indignantly said.

'Doing what?'

'Ordering me around as if I were a halfwit or a child.'

'Sometimes it's the only explanation!' Max took hold of her wrist and walked towards the kitchen, pulling her

after him. 'Sit here, next to the table,' he commanded,
pushing her down on to a chair. He pulled a clean white
towel out of a drawer, and threw it to her. 'Get your
sweater off and drape this around yourself for the
moment.'

She dubiously eyed the towel; it didn't look very big.
Max had found a clean plastic basin; he switched on the
electric kettle, saying to her brusquely, 'This has boiled
once already today, so I just have to reheat it a little.'

He put the basin on the table, switched off the kettle
and poured the hot water into the basin, then went off
to hunt through another cupboard for a bottle of disinfectant, a bag of cotton wool balls, a tin of medical
plasters.

Olivia waited until his back was turned to take off her
sweater, and hurriedly arranged the towel, tucking it
under her arms to cover her from her breasts to her knees.

Squinting down at her shoulder, she saw the circle of
bruising showing already, the smooth tanned skin puffing
up, darkening, with a bleeding graze in the middle of
the circle.

Max frowned at it, moistening cotton wool in the water
cloudy with disinfectant now.

'Why did you say it didn't hurt? It must do.'

He gently began to clean the wound, and she tried not
to wince, closing her eyes. He dried the skin again and
then applied the largest plaster in his tin, a square which
covered most of the bruise.

'Thank you,' she whispered as he dried his hands. She
picked up the sweater to slip it back over her head. Max
took it away from her.

'I'll do that.' But he didn't, not at once. He dropped
it on the table and ran his long index finger down her
naked arm. 'Your skin's as smooth as silk. A pity to be

so rough with it—you should be more careful. Do you always walk into doors?'

Only when she no longer knew her own body space, she thought, only when her full attention was given to running away, instead of looking where she was going.

His finger was trailing on, caressing, tormenting. Her heart was in her throat; she couldn't swallow, or make a sound.

He waited a minute, then bent, very slowly; his lips touched her shoulder, kissing the bruised skin not covered by the plaster.

'So soft,' he muttered. 'Your skin is so soft and cool.'

A slow, sweet, sensual pleasure drowned her mind. She barely breathed, let alone thought. Her eyelids fell over her eyes; her lips quivered in an almost silent groan. His mouth invaded downwards, a conquering army on the march; her breasts were taken, the nipples hard and hot, her pale flesh full and aching.

Max suddenly picked her up from the chair, one hand under her legs, the other under her back.

Olivia's eyes flew open and she looked at him, shaking her head, but not able to speak because fever had possessed her.

Max looked at her quivering mouth. His eyes were hot black coals. Looking into those eyes, she was lost— they set fire to her; she was burning up.

A sound from the doorway startled them both. Max spun around, still holding her.

Christos was crimson, mouth open in a gasp, staring as if he didn't believe his eyes.

When he found his voice it was rough, disgusted. 'So my father was right! He had you last night, you lying little tramp!'

Max stiffened. He put her down into the chair again, moving between her and Christos.

'Get out!' he grated. 'Get out of my house before I lose my temper and knock your teeth down your throat!'

Olivia hurriedly pulled the sweater over her head, dragging it as far as it would go, to her knees, and stood up.

'Stop it, both of you!'

They ignored her. Christos was laughing furiously. 'I'm not afraid of you, damn you!' He came at Max like a whirlwind.

His first blow landed because Max hadn't quite expected him to move so fast. Olivia was sickened by the sound of bone hitting bone: a grinding scrunch, followed by a grunt of pain from Max as he fell backwards.

He stumbled into the wall, and Christos watched, grinning in satisfaction.

'You asked for that!'

Max straightened, face dangerous, and leapt at him across the room. This time it was Christos who was flung backwards. His head collided with the door-frame and he fell full-length like a tree brought down by an axe.

Appalled, Olivia waited for him to get up again, but he didn't. He lay there with his eyes closed, not moving.

'Oh, my God, you may have killed him!' Olivia said, running forward to kneel beside Christos.

As she looked at him his lashes fluttered, his eyes blinked and opened, he looked at her dazedly, then his eyes opened wider, recognising her, and he scowled.

'Are you all right?' she asked anxiously.

He put a hand to his jaw, explored inside his mouth with his tongue, and grimaced, his face sulky. 'I think one of my teeth is loose, otherwise I'm all in one piece.'

He glared at her and then at Max. 'Sorry to disappoint you, you didn't kill me.'

'Oh, stop it, Christos, don't be so childish!' Olivia burst out, getting up.

He got to his feet too, shakily, pulling away when she tried to help him. 'Leave me alone.'

'I thought I told you and your father to get off my island?' Max put a possessive arm around Olivia and jerked her against his side, keeping his arm around her.

Christos watched, brows heavy over his sullen eyes.

'We're going at once, don't worry. Before we sailed, I had the stupid idea that I ought to make quite sure Olivia wouldn't prefer to come with us, just in case the helicopter doesn't get back in time.' Christos laughed unpleasantly. 'Funny, really, isn't it? My chivalrous gestures always end up as jokes. Sorry I bothered you both when you were having such fun. Forget I interrupted.'

He turned on his heel and left, staggering slightly on his way to the front door.

'You didn't have to hit him so hard!' Olivia said, moving to follow him to make sure he was OK. Max refused to let go of her, his arm tightening.

'I didn't have to, no! I wanted to!' Max said, his eyes full of smouldering temper. 'He wasn't calling you a filthy name and getting away with it! Even if it had been true, he wouldn't have been justified in calling you that!'

'You can't blame him for thinking the worst of me, after what he saw just now!'

'Feeling guilty, Olivia?' Max asked drily, and she wished he wasn't so quick and shrewd.

'I was engaged to him——' she began, and Max cut her off with an impatient gesture.

'Don't start that again. We've been through that too many times already. You have no reason to feel guilty over Christos. It's only his pride that hurts, not his heart. Now, if you want to get in touch with your mother I suggest you do so now before the helicopter arrives. They shouldn't be much longer.'

He strode out of the kitchen and she followed him into the radio room again and watched him sit down and start operating the set.

'Sit here,' he commanded in that peremptory way of his a moment or two later. 'It's ringing.'

It was strange to hear her mother's voice, coming through a faint crackle of static electricity.

'Mum, it's Olivia,' she said, and her mother exclaimed in surprise.

'Where are you ringing from? You sound very far away.'

'I'm on Hymnos.'

'Where?'

'The island that was being auctioned, remember? I told you, that was why we came to Greece, to buy Hymnos.'

'I remember that, I just didn't remember the name. So, did they buy it?'

'No. Listen, Mum, something's happened—it isn't good news, I'm afraid. Dad's had a heart attack.'

She heard the inhalation of breath at the other end. 'Is it serious?'

'I don't know yet. They've flown him to hospital, and I'll be going there too shortly. I'll keep in touch and let you know how he is.'

'Yes, do that,' her mother said slowly. 'Are you OK, darling? You sound odd. It must have been a terrible shock for you too. Is Christos looking after you?'

'The engagement's off, Mum,' Olivia said huskily.

'What did you say? This line is so bad, I thought you said...'

'I'm not going to marry Christos,' Olivia repeated.

'That was what I thought you said! What on earth has been happening, Olivia? No, never mind—look, shall I come out there? Or don't you want me?'

'Oh, I'd love you to, Mum,' Olivia said gratefully. 'I didn't like to ask, but if you could... Could you get away?'

'I'll manage, leave it to me. Do I fly to Athens? Where is this hospital? How far is it from Athens? How would I get there?'

Olivia looked at Max who leaned forward and spoke into the microphone. 'Mrs Faulton... this is Max Agathios. I imagine you know who I am...'

'Yes,' her mother said, sounding even more startled. 'Of course, Mr Agathios.'

'I suggest that I book you on to a flight from Heathrow to Athens, and I'll meet your plane and take you to the hospital.'

'That's very thoughtful of you, Mr Agathios, and I'd be grateful if I could be met, but there's no need for you to book my flight for me too.'

'Mrs Faulton, I intend to be your son-in-law—please permit me to do this small service for you,' Max said formally.

Olivia stiffened, pale and then flushing angrily. How dared he?

Her mother audibly gasped. 'Oh. Oh, I see. At least, I don't, but... Well, it can wait until I see Olivia and find out exactly what's been going on over there!'

Max laughed shortly. 'Good. Now, I'll get my secretary to book your flight and get in touch to let you know the timings. I'll be waiting when you come out of the Customs area. I'll carry a board with your name written on it.'

Overhead they heard the sound of the helicopter whirring through the sky, and Max shot Olivia a glance, sat back and gestured for her to finish the call.

'Mum, I've got to go now, but I'll see you soon,' she said stiffly.

'I can't wait to see you and find out what on earth you've been up to!' her mother said in a dry voice.

Olivia's heart sank. Her mother was going to put her through a tough interrogation as soon as they were alone. Olivia didn't look forward to it.

Max ended the call as Olivia got up from her chair. She watched, glaring at him. When he got up too she snapped, 'How dare you tell my mother that?'

'Why shouldn't she know? She'll have to know sooner or later, or aren't you going to ask her to our wedding?'

'We aren't having a wedding!'

He pretended to be shocked, opening his dark eyes wide. 'No wedding? Olivia, I'm old-fashioned, I couldn't just live with you without marrying you.'

'You know perfectly well what I meant! You aren't marrying me just to get my father's shares in your company!'

'I don't need them,' he said, a glitter of excitement in his face. 'Events have moved on very fast today—while the medical people were loading your father on to the helicopter I came in here to check if there were any messages waiting for me, and found one, asking me to call an old friend.'

'Who?' she asked, his excited tone alerting her. Not Daphne Kera, surely? Jealousy niggled inside her chest. She watched him tensely, and Max grinned at her.

'He's a rival, actually, George Korsavo; his shipping company isn't as big as mine but it has some interesting contracts. It has been growing steadily for the last few years, and, most importantly, he owns it outright. He never went public; nobody else has any shares. He's older than me, in his late forties, and he only has two daughters and a son. Both girls are married, and have no interest in the firm, and his only son has never been interested in shipping. George heard I'd been forced off my board so he rang me to ask if I'd be interested in becoming managing director of his company. He's diversifying—he has bought into a private airfield and acquired a small private airline. His boy, Ioannis, is crazy about flying and works as a pilot; he persuaded his father to buy an airline for him but Ioannis isn't interested in the business side, just in the flying, at the moment. George can't give the same time and attention to both companies—he needs a partner, someone with money, someone he can trust, to take over the shipping side and run that for him. He asked me if I'd be interested, and I jumped at it.'

She frowned, 'But it won't be your own company!'

'I'll have a considerable share of it—I'm investing every penny I can raise.'

'But you aren't selling your island?'

'I have sold it,' he said, and her golden eyes opened even wider. 'Privately, to a Japanese buyer who wants to make it a holiday resort, build hotels and luxury holiday villas. The estate agent advised me to accept the offer, and cancel the auction. The new buyer refused to enter into an auction—if I didn't accept his offer he would withdraw, and his offer was so huge that I had to agree with the agent. I couldn't believe anyone else would pay that much. I was thinking it over when I got the call from George, so I told him yes, and then I rang the agent and told him to close the deal with the Japanese firm, then rang my stockbrokers and told them to start selling my shares in my own company. I'll need a lot of money to buy a partnership with George.'

'So you're pulling out of your own company altogether?' she slowly said and he shrugged.

'Constantine wants it—let him have it!'

'But...I'm confused,' she said. 'You told Constantine you'd see him in the boardroom very soon...and you told me you thought you would probably get your company back...'

'I don't want to give my brother any early warnings. If I'm to sell my shares at the top price I have to do it quickly, without anyone knowing what is going on.'

She saw the point of that. 'OK,' she conceded. 'But why let me think you were still hoping to get your company back?'

He shot her a dry look. 'You were so busy thinking the worst, I let you go ahead and do it. I was angry with you, I suppose, for being ready to listen to Christos and my brother, ready to believe their accusations. When are you going to start thinking for yourself, trusting your own judgement?'

He was right about that too, she couldn't deny it. Watching him uncertainly, she asked, 'But...won't you mind? I mean, your father left the company to you, and you built it up... Isn't it going to be hard to lose it?'

'What I did once I can do again,' Max said, his eyes bright. 'It's a challenge, and I love challenges! My father would approve, I'm sure of that. All he left me was a few old ships which won't last much longer anyway.' He laughed. 'They won't do Constantine much good. It wasn't them he was fixated on—he coveted them only because he was so jealous of me; he never forgave our

'ather for having another son. You know, once I've sold
my shares the share price will drop, and Constantine is
going to have a problem. The shareholders, not to
mention the other directors, are going to be furious, and
hey'll blame Constantine.'

She couldn't feel much pity for his half-brother. 'I'd
like to be a fly on the wall when he discovers what you've
done!' she said slowly.

Max laughed. 'So would I!'

They flew away ten minutes later into the glorious
sunlight of an autumn morning. Staring down at the blue
Aegean, Olivia found it hard to believe that so much
had happened since she arrived in Athens.

It was only a couple of days ago, yet she felt as if she
had experienced a whole lifetime, crowded with incident.

She spent hours in the hospital, waiting to see her
father. Max made a number of phone calls, out of
earshot, but he rarely took his eyes off her, and she
couldn't deny she found his constant presence
comforting.

He told her his secretary had only been able to book
her mother on to the first flight next day. 'She will arrive
around noon. I'll meet her, as I promised. Stop looking
worried, Olivia, it is going to be OK—your father is in
good hands.'

'I hope so,' she said fervently.

At last she was allowed to see her father, but alone,
although Max walked with her to the door of the private
room. Gerald Faulton lay on the bed, his chest bare but
a cover pulled up over him. Its white weave made his
skin look very grey, his lips were still blue, but she fancied
he looked just a little better than he had; there was a
trace of colour in his face and his eyes were clearer.

'I'm sorry to give you a scare, Dad, and cause all thi
trouble,' she said, holding his hand.

Weakly, he murmured, 'Don't be silly. I'm just gla
you're alive.'

'Same here,' she said, pressing his fingers, and smile
waveringly.

He looked down at her hand. 'No ring,' he whispered
and she bit her lip.

'No.' She hadn't meant to tell him yet, in case it upse
him.

'Did you end it?'

She nodded, watching him uneasily, but he didn't seer
disturbed, or even surprised.

'It's Max, isn't it?' her father said in that dry, wea
voice, and after a moment's hesitation she nodded
Gerald Faulton sighed, gave a pale smile. 'As long a
you're happy.' He swallowed, and whispered, 'When
thought…you were dead…it hit me badly, Olivia. You'r
all I have in the world and I thought I'd lost you.'

Her eyes stung with tears.

Later, the specialist looking after him told her, 'It wa
a minor heart attack, but it was a warning. He mus
change his lifestyle if he wants to survive—he must tak
things easier, not work so hard…'

She laughed shakily. 'Shall I tell him, or will you? H
isn't going to listen either way.'

'If he doesn't, I can't predict a future for him,' th
man said grimly. 'He must stop drinking, stop smokin;
take more exercise. And I'll tell him so, I assure yo
Now, I suggest you get a good night's rest, Miss Faulto
you look very tired.'

Wearily she walked along the highly polished hospit
corridor towards the exit, Max's hand under her elbo
as if he was afraid to let go of her in case she fell ove

She felt as if she might, too; she had never been so tired
in her life. It was only as they walked out into a soft
dusk light that it dawned on her that her problems
weren't over yet.

'Can you recommend a discreet hotel?' she asked Max.
'My luggage is all on the yacht, including my money,
credit cards and passport. How am I going to get them
back?'

'The yacht was heading for Piraeus. I'm sure
Constantine will have someone pack up your things, and
he'll bring them to the hospital tomorrow—he's bound
to visit your father. As for a hotel, don't worry. I'll take
you to the most sympathetic hotel I know.'

He had had a car waiting when they flew here earlier,
which was parked in the hospital car park. She sank into
the passenger seat and shut her eyes; Max started the
engine and drove off. Olivia was so tired she almost fell
asleep then. She woke with a start as they shot down
into an underground car park.

'Where are we?' she asked, looking dazedly around.

'The hotel I told you about,' said Max, coming round
to help her out of the car.

They went up in a lift from the car park; Olivia leaned
on the steel wall, staring at her own reflection opposite:
a blurred image with yellow hair and a white face, a
ghostly wraith in a strange, very short dress.

'No hotel will let me in looking like this!' she wailed.

'This one will,' said Max, grinning at her as the lift
stopped.

She walked out, looked around, expecting to see a
hotel lobby, but found herself in a wide corridor with a
polished floor.

'Where is this?'

Max steered her towards the end of the corridor. 'Thi
way.' He produced a key and unlocked a door, and Olivi
backed, shaking her head, angrily turning pink.

'I am not sharing your room! I want a room of m
own!'

Max put an arm round her waist and lifted her off th
ground, carried her inside the door and kicked it shu
with one foot, leaving them in darkness.

'Let me out of here!' Olivia yelled, trying to brea
free of his grip. It was useless, of course. Max hoiste
her up over his shoulder in a fireman's lift, and switche
on the light. Her head hanging down, she found hersel
staring at a tiled floor; she twisted to get a view of wall
papered in a pretty ivy-covered design.

Max opened a door on the left, switched on anothe
light, and she had a disorientating glimpse of a bedroom
all cool colours: blue curtains, a blue and white carpet
a white bed. In spite of the stark simplicity there was a
elegance and style which made it obvious that his déco
had cost a great deal of money. She had never seen
hotel that looked like this.

'This isn't a hotel, is it?' she asked as Max droppe
her unceremoniously on the bed. His face looked di
turbingly grim, angular, set.

'It's my flat,' he said. 'This is my bed, and you a
my woman.'

Her body jerked into fierce life, her pulses beatin
under her skin, her nerves jumping.

'No, Max, I won't, it wouldn't work out—after every
thing that's happened, we wouldn't be happy together
she wailed, panic-stricken by the look in his eyes.

'I've waited for five years,' he said harshly. 'I hurt
man I admired very much, and owed an enormous det
to—I hurt his daughter, by jilting her for you. An

eventually you cost me my company when Daphne sold her shares to Constantine and your father. I'm not complaining, Olivia—I'd do it all again tomorrow. You can't set a price tag on love. But don't tell me we wouldn't be happy together. Because I know I can't be happy without you. I don't want to live without you for even one more day.'

He pushed her down against the pillows and leaned over her, his face inches away, and she suddenly heard the wild racing of his heart. Or was it her own heart beating in that overheated way?

'I need you, Olivia,' he muttered, staring at her mouth. 'Tell me you need me too.'

She stared back, her mouth going dry, her body hot.

'Don't torment me,' he whispered. 'Say it—let me make love to you before I go out of my mind.'

'Can I stop you?' she asked, torn between wanting him and the fear that too much stood between them.

'You just have to say no,' Max said, his face even grimmer. 'You told me last night that you couldn't make love because you weren't free, you were still engaged to Christos, and I accepted that—in fact, I admired your principles. I find it hard to forgive my half-brother because he coveted my company—I had to be honest enough to admit I had no right to covet you while you were engaged to my nephew, even though I was certain you didn't love him, and he wasn't in love with you either. But you had given him your word—I respected that. But you aren't engaged any more. Forget your father, and my half-brother, and business. Forget everything that's happened lately. This is just you and me now.' He touched her cheek with one finger lingeringly, his eyes tender and passionate. 'I love you, Olivia. Will you marry me?'

She closed her eyes and stopped fighting the inevitable. She had known this would happen, ever since she saw him again, that day in her father's office when Max exploded into the room and blew her safe, carefully arranged life to pieces.

He was right: the only thing that mattered was the way he made her feel, the passion that she felt, now, vibrating between them. There were just the two of them in the world tonight, and Olivia wanted him more than she had ever wanted anything in her entire life; her body cried out for him, hungered for him, now. Now. And forever.

'Yes, Max,' she said.

HARLEQUIN PRESENTS®

Just a taste!

Sample the exciting new story from top author
Jacqueline Baird:

#1827 *A Devious Desire*

"Wait, Alex.... Marriage is a big step—are you sure
you're ready for it? You have been a bachelor for an
awful long time."

"Marriage? Who mentioned marriage?" He let go of
her and stepped back as if he had been stung.

"I'm sorry if I misunderstood," she said softly, acting for
all she was worth. "But I'm afraid that's the only way
you'll ever get me."

Will Saffron snare Alex and get her revenge?

Available in August wherever Harlequin books are sold.

TAUTH-11

MILLION DOLLAR SWEEPSTAKES

THIS TIME, FOREVER

Four years ago Darcy made a pass at heartthrob
Keir Robards. And he turned her down flat.

BUT
NOW
HE'S
BACK!

And Darcy is determined to make him pay....

#1831 FAST AND LOOSE
by Elizabeth Oldfield

Available in August wherever
Harlequin books are sold.

HARLEQUIN PRESENTS®

HARLEQUIN PRESENTS®

Ties of Passion
by Sally Wentworth

The story of the Brodey family. Money, looks, style—the
Brodeys have everything...except love.

Read part one of this exciting three-part series

#1832 CHRIS

Chris Brodey could offer Tiffany anything she wanted,
but she soon discovered that he wasn't a man prepared to
give something for nothing....

**Watch for books two and three in
September and October!**

Available in August wherever Harlequin books are sold.

TOPG

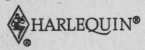